ARQuiz# 86095
BL: 5.5
ARPts: 8.0

THE
SECRET
PRINCE

Also by D. Anne Love

The Puppeteer's Apprentice
Margaret K. McElderry Books

- THE -
SECRET
PRINCE

D. ANNE LOVE

Margaret K. McElderry Books
New York   London   Toronto   Sydney

Margaret K. McElderry Books
An imprint of Simon & Schuster
Children's Publishing Division
1230 Avenue of the Americas
New York, New York 10020

Book design by Ann Zeak
The text for this book is set in Italian Garamond.

Manufactured in the United States of America
2 4 6 8 10 9 7 5 3 1
Library of Congress Cataloging-in-Publication Data
Love, D. Anne.
The secret prince / D. Anne Love.—1st ed.
p. cm.
Summary: Informed at the age of twelve that he is the long-awaited prince of Kelhadden, Thorn sets off on a quest to find the magical amulet that will enable him to dethrone the evil usurper, Ranulf.
ISBN 0-689-84426-3 (hardcover)
[1. Adventure and adventurers—Fiction. 2. Princes—Fiction. 3. Magic—Fiction. 4. Twins—Fiction. 5. Fairy tales.] I. Title.
PZ7.L9549Se 2005
[Fic]—dc22
2003026395

FIRST
EDITION

In memory of my father, who taught me to love books.
I miss you, Daddy.

Acknowledgments

With love and thanks to the California Girls: Ann Collins, Donna Guthrie, and Christy Zatkin; to my family and to Leanna Ellis for holding my hand in good times and bad; and as always, to Emma Dryden for her wisdom, patience, and unfailing support. I am blessed.

Old men and comets have been reverenced
for the same reason; their long beards,
and pretenses to foretell events.
—Jonathan Swift

CHAPTER ONE

AT FIRST MORWID COULDN'T SAY WHAT HAD AWAKENED
him. One moment he was dreaming peacefully of his
old life in the castle, the next he was wide awake, his
failing eyes straining against the darkness of the sea
cave.

Drawing his blanket around his shoulders, he sat up,
listening for any sound of approaching danger, but all
was quiet, save the trills of the forest creatures and the
crashing of the sea against the rocky shore below.

He lit a torch and moved to the opening of the cave.
Above him the night sky glowed with the color of blood.
Along the horizon a sphere of light pulsed and grew
until it blotted out all the stars. As if launched from a

huntsman's bow, it arced across the heavens, trailing fire, then disappeared in a shimmer of gold that briefly lit the dark sea.

The old warrior trembled with hope and longing. "When the heavens are red with fire, he will come," he whispered. "So say the prophets."

He ran his fingers along the rocky ledge above the entrance to the cave till they touched the prize he had guarded since fleeing the castle so many years before. The Book of Ancients held spells and stories, curses and cures, promises and prophecies for the kingdom of Kelhadden. Morwid took it down and clutched it to his chest. He had no need to read it now; he knew every page by heart. But the weight of it, and the smell of leather, dust, and secrets mingling in the air, comforted him.

Too anxious for sleep, he stood for a moment holding the book until his hands and heart steadied, then he returned the tome to its place. He stoked the fire that burned day and night against the chill of the cave and set his blackened water pot on the coals. While the water heated, he opened a pouch and measured into a bowl a pinch of bloodrose and a dusting of dried balsam leaves. Muttering to himself, he upended the entire contents of a second pouch into his bowl. "Plenty of sage," he murmured, "for I shall surely need all my wisdom when he comes."

Morwid poured the bubbling water over the herbs and, when the mixture had cooled, drank it down. Then he laced his leggings, picked up his fishing line and basket, and left the cave.

The sky had lightened to an ordinary shade of gray; the rising sun was a seam of fire on the horizon. Atop the farthest promontory stood the castle at Kelhadden. Sheltered by a thick growth of alders and oaks, its granite turrets and towers glittered in the growing light. High on the roof a red-and-yellow banner danced in the morning breeze.

Morwid set off toward the sea, moving carefully, for the trail to the bottom of the cliff was treacherous with sharp crags and hidden drops where the unwary could tumble to certain death. Though he was slow of step, his thoughts were agile as ever, darting from one question to another. When would the promised one arrive? Would he come alone or with a legion of warriors? Would he allow Morwid to accompany him to the castle? This thought brought a smile to the old warrior's face, for he had long dreamed of standing sword to sword with Ranulf on the day when the odious Northman was ousted at last.

Though many years had passed since Ranulf had overrun Kelhadden and seized the entire kingdom for himself and his kinsmen, Morwid's memory of the humiliating defeat he had suffered that bitter winter was still rapier sharp. A desire for revenge burned in his gut like fire. Now the comet and the red sky promised deliverance. Buoyed by the prospect of his imminent return to the castle, Morwid felt neither the pains in his knees nor the sharp stones beneath his feet as he made his way to the shore.

He reached the sand and cast his line into the rolling waves. The first rays of morning sun penetrated the depths of the sea cliffs and cast a golden glow across the water. The smells of salt and kelp hung heavy in the air. As fine a day as any for a trip to the village, he mused. Though Morwid detested traveling in disguise, he still had a price on his head, and the ravaged village was rife with Ranulf's spies. But today, eager for news of the comet and the one it promised, he was willing to brave any danger.

When his basket brimmed with fish, Morwid coiled his line and began the slow walk home. Near twilight, as he neared the cave, a strange wailing halted his steps. Unsure whether the sound was human or animal, he warily crossed the clearing, then stopped short. At the entrance to the cave sat a basket made of reeds. Inside it lay an infant, wrinkled, red faced, and howling.

"By my bones!" Morwid cried aloud. "Who has brought this babe to my door?"

He rushed inside his cave and anxiously surveyed his belongings. All his herbs and potions were lined up neatly along their ledge. The fire danced merrily inside its circle of stones. The Book of Ancients lay undisturbed just where he had left it.

The infant's cry grew louder and so full of anguish that Morwid hurried to the basket, lifted the child, and began to sing an ancient song he had learned as a boy. Though the old warrior's voice was rusty from disuse, the babe quieted and nestled against Morwid's shoulder. "Aye. 'Tis better now," he crooned. "I know not who left you here, or why, but you cannot stay. Why, just this morn came a sign from the heavens. As clear a portent as ever I have seen. The prince of Kelhadden is on his way at last, and I must be ready."

He shifted the infant to his other arm. "Oh, little one, you cannot imagine how long I have waited and hoped for this day. So you see, though you be a pitiful mite, I cannot look after you. There is important work to be done."

Something warm and wet ran down Morwid's sleeve. The child stirred and began to fuss again.

"By the saints, you have wet on me!" Morwid laid the babe in the basket and heaved an exasperated sigh. Soon it would be too late to start for the village. Besides, he couldn't leave a wet, hungry infant alone in the cave, at the mercy of prowling animals. On the morrow he would leave the child at the village church. Then he would see whether there was news of the prince.

The babe let out another lusty wail.

"Patience!" Morwid muttered. "Or I shall leave you to wallow in your own piss."

He rummaged through his few belongings for dry swaddling and settled upon the cloth sack he used for carrying provisions to and from the village. He bent over the basket and loosened the damp, sour-smelling blanket. The babe blinked and watched the old man solemnly. When the swaddling fell away, Morwid's hands stilled. Words of the ancients sprang unbidden to his mind as he regarded the child's tuft of tawny hair and wide, amber-colored eyes:

> *Strong of bone and fair of face,*
> *the prince shall take his rightful place.*
> *Golden hair and golden eye,*
> *such are signs to know him by.*

"Nay," Morwid said aloud. "By my bones, it cannot be!"

A bubble rose in his throat that was very nearly a sob. He had expected the promised prince to arrive all grown up, with strong limbs and an even stronger heart. Nothing less would defeat Ranulf and the Northmen. But now Morwid remembered another part of the prophecy:

> *From one who is wise,*
> *though he be old,*

*the prince must hear
his story told.
And then to rise, his powers known,
to claim at last his rightful throne.*

Stunned, Morwid wrapped the babe in the dry cloth and sat down to ponder the day's events. If this infant truly *were* the prince, it would be years before he could claim his kingdom. The child *seemed* to be the one the Book of Ancients described; on the other hand, all the Northmen were robust and fair haired. Perhaps the babe had been left at the cave purely by chance by a mother unable to care for him.

The babe cried out. Morwid stood and took some comfrey from his store of herbs. He was in dire need of a calming potion, for this squalling child had disrupted the peace he depended upon. Of late his mind seemed to return more and more often to his early years in Kelhadden. Memories were his greatest comfort during the long evenings, and he took them out one by one, like jewels from a box, each one a shining reminder of what had once been and what might have been. He resented anything that interrupted his reveries. Still, the arrival of the golden-eyed boy child on the very night of the red sky must mean something.

"Drucilla." He spoke her name aloud, with the same affection as in the days of their youth in Kelhadden. "I will take this babe to her, and together we will sort things out."

The child yawned and turned his head, and Morwid noticed a red tricornered mark, no larger than his thumbnail, behind the baby's ear. It reminded him of the thicket of briers clinging to the great stone wall at Kelhadden.

"I shall name you Thorn," he decided, "for want of a better name."

The babe blinked his golden eyes, soaked his swaddling again, and bellowed long and loudly for his dinner. Morwid made a broth of fish and herbs and spooned it into the child's mouth drop by drop. While the babe slept, Morwid sipped his comfrey brew, made ready for their journey, then stretched out beside the flickering fire.

Birdsong woke Morwid before sunrise, and he set off with the infant still asleep in his wet swaddling.

Morwid picked his way along the path that led down to the forest, fitting his steps into the ridges of the trail. The sky lightened, until he could see the bright glitter of the distant sea and, far below, the cool green woods where Drucilla lived in a wattle-and-daub hut far too mean for a woman of her gifts. Near midday, as he neared the hut, he shifted the infant and quickened his pace. Though it would pain his friend to do what he would ask her, his hopes for the future of Kelhadden depended upon it.

Soon he arrived at Drucilla's hut, where he rapped three times, waited, then rapped again.

The door opened. A hand emerged, grabbed his sleeve, and drew him inside. Morwid was stunned at how thin Drucilla had grown since their last chance meeting some months earlier. Her dark hair, once lustrous as a raven's wing, had gone gray, and her arms and legs seemed lost in the folds of her blue robes. But her voice was strong as she greeted him. "Morwid! My dear friend! I woke this morning knowing you would come." She drew back the swaddling. "By my faith. This child is wet as winter on the moors. He must be changed and fed. Then we will talk."

While Drucilla bustled about the hut tending the infant, Morwid recounted his sighting of the red sky and the mysterious appearance of the golden-eyed child. "The Book of Ancients . . . ," he began.

"Aye." Drucilla settled the child on a blanket before the fire. "It is sometimes maddening in its vagueness, but it served our king well till the very end, did it not?"

"Not well enough," Morwid muttered. "Had he heeded its warning, or listened to my counsel, our kingdom would not have been lost."

"King Warn was but a mortal," Drucilla said quietly. "Even the gods are not immune to vanity and the desires of their own hearts."

The infant began to fuss. Morwid picked him up,

stuck his own finger into the child's mouth, and rocked to and fro till Thorn quieted.

Drucilla grinned in a way that made her seem almost young again. "By all the saints, Morwid, I do believe you missed your calling. All this time we thought you a brave and wise warrior, a counselor to kings, when 'tis plain you were meant to be a nursemaid."

Long ago Morwid would have enjoyed her banter, but today his eyes were gritty from lack of sleep and his thoughts far too troubled. "Drucilla—"

She stopped him with an uplifted hand. "You need not ask. What kind of seer would I be if I could not divine why you have come?"

"I would spare you the pain if I could, but I must know whether this boy be the true prince of Kelhadden."

"Aye." She took a brown clay pot from a shelf. "Lay him here by the hearth, then fill this vessel from the rain barrel beside the door. But be mindful of the Northmen. I heard them this morn long before the cock's first crow, riding toward the sea."

Morwid went for the water and returned to find Drucilla seated on a low stool. Beside her was a table covered with a green cloth, upon which sat a circle of stubby, unlit candles and a ball of amber glass. She waited while Morwid set the water before her and seated himself opposite her. Then Drucilla waved her hand above the candles. A circle of flame sprang up, making a small island of flickering yellow light inside the dim hut. Cupping her hands around the pot, the seer closed her eyes and chanted:

> *"Fire and water, air and earth,*
> *reveal the truth of this child's birth."*

Drucilla opened her eyes. She passed her hand over the water, and the ripples followed her fingers as if drawn by a magnet. "Now we will see what we will see," she whispered.

Wrinkling her brow, the seer peered into the still water. Morwid clutched the edge of the table and watched his friend anxiously across the dancing flames. Outside, the wind rustled in the vines. A bare branch knocked against the window. The silence lengthened till Morwid at last cried, "Well?"

Drucilla shook her head, her expression troubled. She rubbed her eyes and pushed the water away. "Perhaps these old eyes fail me at last. Or else my gift itself is waning. I fear you have journeyed here for naught, my friend. I cannot say for certain whether this child is the one."

"I must know! Try your scrying glass."

With a resigned sigh Drucilla picked up the amber ball and bent over it. Soon her face contorted. A sheen of sweat filmed her forehead. She moaned and took several ragged breaths. "Ahh. Two there be," she whispered at last. "One alone, then two as one, until at last the quest be done."

Morwid snatched the glass. The candles went out. "Two as one?" he cried into the darkness. "What does it mean?"

Drucilla raised her head. "I am certain of nothing save this: The prince, whoever he be, must find the lost amulet that lies far beyond the summer country. In the amulet lies the power to oust the Northmen. But there will be much pain in the taking of it."

"Where is it exactly?"

"Beyond water and fire. Beyond ice. Beyond the raging wind."

Morwid paced the little hut. "What am I to do? I am far too old to waste my final years preparing a boy who might or might not be the one the ancients have promised." He stopped his pacing and placed a hand on Drucilla's shoulder. "And the pain you spoke of. Is there no way around it? Surely there must be some spell or enchantment that will do the trick."

"Some of my sisters can call up fire and rain, some can stop the wind. It is said my mother's gifts were strong enough to stop time." Drucilla took both of Morwid's hands in hers. "The years grow long, so perhaps you have forgotten that mine has always been a minor gift. I am but a seer, powerless to change what fate ordains."

Morwid opened his mouth to speak, but she silenced him with a finger to her lips. "I am tired now, and hungry. Let us eat before the child wakes and you must journey home."

So saying, she opened a cupboard and took out a crust of barley bread, some comb honey, and a bit of cheese. Stepping silently around the sleeping Thorn, she poured a watery ale into two goblets, and they sat down to eat.

They spoke then of the old days in Kelhadden, when they were young and the walls of the castle rang with music and laughter. They spoke of cool green gardens and summers by the sea, and of good friends long dead but hardly forgotten. They spoke of Morwid's dream of the future, when the Northmen would be banished from Kelhadden forever. Morwid lifted his goblet. "To the prince," he said. "Wherever and whoever he be!"

"To the prince." Drucilla drained her ale and stood. "It will be dark soon, and I do not like to imagine you in this wood then. The king's huntsmen would as soon spear you as the stag. You must go now, but I will give you more swaddling for the boy." She shook her head. "The poor mite needs milk, but I have none."

"Aye. It would be easier to call down rain than to find any while Ranulf forbids us our own animals."

Drucilla lifted Thorn from his makeshift bed and removed his swaddling. Morwid held his nose against the acrid smell, but the seer seemed not to notice. She wrapped Thorn in dry blankets and dribbled a bit of gruel left from her breakfast into his mouth. The babe sucked her finger greedily and closed his eyes. Drucilla rocked the child and looked up at Morwid, her black eyes glistening with tears. "Mayhap this day I have held our new prince."

"And mayhap you have not." Morwid sighed and stroked his beard. "If only I could be certain."

"My counsel is this: Proceed as if this babe *is* the prince. Teach him everything he must know in order to find the lost amulet. When he reaches his twelfth summer, bring him to me. Perhaps then I can divine his true calling."

"A wasted effort," Morwid grumbled, "to teach him all I know only to find he is nothing but a worthless foundling."

"Learning is never wasted," Drucilla said. "If he is not the prince, at least you will have a well-trained lad to aid you and to ease the loneliness of your cave." She placed the sleeping child in Morwid's arms. "I worry about you, my friend, living alone in such a cold, dark place."

Morwid grunted. "I am a warrior. I have seen worse. This hut of yours is hardly better. When Ranulf is defeated, I will come down and make you a proper house."

Drucilla laughed. "We are both too old for such an undertaking, but I thank you just the same." She opened the door and peered out. "All clear. But watch how you go."

The old warrior kissed her cheek and slipped into the fading light. He had not meant to stay so late. Already the sun lay low in the trees, casting long shadows along the forest floor. His mind teemed with questions. Was this babe the prince who would someday reclaim the kingdom? Or was he merely the castoff of some desperate woman who had chanced upon the cave? If Thorn *were* the prince, what should he be taught for a journey beyond fire and wind and ice? Hunting and fishing, aye, and how to read the stars. Swordsmanship and archery. Riding? But where would Morwid get a horse when such animals were forbidden to all but Ranulf's men? Just as worrisome was Drucilla's odd pronouncement. *Two as one.* What could it mean? He turned it over in his mind, but still it made no sense.

So busy were his thoughts that the huntsmen were nearly upon him before he realized the danger. The thunder of horses' hooves shook the ground. Then the red-cloaked king himself, riding a magnificent black stallion, crashed through the trees, his huntsmen and baying hounds following. Behind them ran two hollow-eyed men, ragged and barefoot, calling out to the king, begging for the entrails of the hares dangling from the huntsmen's horses. The cracking of horsewhips, followed by the anguished cries of the beggars, filled the air. Morwid hid behind a tree and cradled Thorn to his chest. He felt his familiar hatred for the Northmen returning. Once, those poor beggars had been men of substance, farmers perhaps, or farriers or merchants or millers. But Ranulf had pillaged the entire kingdom and forced all but the most despairing of his subjects into hiding.

Swallowing the rage roiling inside him, Morwid waited for the Northmen and the beggars to pass, then ran deeper into the forest, until he reached the edge of a dark pond. There he crouched in the damp reeds and covered the baby's body with his own. Thorn whimpered, and Morwid put his lips to the baby's ear and quieted him with the words of one old song and then another until the sounds of men, dogs, and horses faded. Morwid lifted his head and looked around. He was bone tired. The sea cave was too far away to reach before nightfall, and he was unwilling to chance another encounter with the hunting party in order to return to Drucilla's hut. With a sinking heart he realized he and the babe must wait in the forest until morning.

The coming night promised to be a cold one. He

could smell the frost, and the wood smoke from the far-off huts of the forest people. Without tools for fire making, he could do nothing except huddle with the infant in the tall grass. He wrapped Thorn in all the swaddling Drucilla had provided, then held the child close inside his own cloak. The warrior and the infant warmed each other as the moon rose through the bare tree branches and the wind soughed in the reeds beside the pond.

"Did I ever tell you about the time King Warn and I, with only a handful of men, held off the king of Arnen for nearly a week?" Morwid asked the babe. "Aye, and it was a fierce battle, to be sure, as we had to rely more on our wits than our skills with dirk and lance, there being so few of us, you see. 'Tis better to use one's head than to lose it to the enemy's poleax."

The sound of his own voice comforted the old warrior, and so he went on with his tales until he and the child both fell asleep.

CHAPTER TWO

"AWAKE, BOY!"

With the toe of his sandal Morwid nudged Thorn's shoulder till the boy started and sat up, rubbing his eyes. At nearly seven, Thorn was tall for his age and strong limbed from clambering over the steep trails and trotting after Morwid everywhere the old warrior went.

"What will we do today?" Thorn asked, yawning. "I should like to practice setting my snares. I nearly caught a quail yestermorn."

"Nearly is not good enough. A lesson you will learn for yourself when your belly is empty as a church on Monday." Morwid handed Thorn a ragged brown garment. "No hunting today. Don this robe and come outside. We must go to the village at Kelhadden."

Kelhadden! Thorn could recall only one other time—when he was no more than four or five—that the old man had taken him from the seclusion of the cave to the village far below. That day Morwid, full of dire warnings about the giant Northmen who had taken over the entire kingdom, bundled Thorn into a scratchy, hooded robe and forbade him to speak a single word. Thorn had traveled with Morwid under cover of night, and an old woman in long blue robes had let them into her hut and given them a few provisions.

Thorn remembered the excitement of the secret trip, running alongside Morwid in the dark, the smell of wet leaves and moss giving way as they neared the town to the stench of human waste and garbage rotting in the streets. He remembered the shouts of the ironmongers and the *clip-clop* of the Northmen's horses' hooves seeming thunderous after the quiet of the cave. Most vivid was the memory of Morwid's furtive expression and his whispered conversations with men who pretended not to know him whenever anyone else approached. Aye, that and the memory of the warm honey cakes with raisins they had eaten on the way home. Mayhap there would be another honey cake at the end of this day's journey. Thorn's mouth watered at the prospect of such a rare treat.

He slipped the tunic over his head and followed Morwid outside, rubbing his arms against the morning's bitter chill. It was still early; daylight dribbled through the gray mist hanging above the sea.

"Bend over and hold still." Morwid took up a pitcher of warm black liquid and, before Thorn knew quite what was happening, poured it over Thorn's head, dyeing his yellow hair to a dirty-looking brown.

"Teacher, why—," Thorn began.

"The village is a dangerous place. You know that." Morwid dried his hands and spun Thorn around, inspecting his handiwork. "That yellow hair of yours shines like a torch. But no one will take notice of a harmless old priest and his mousy-looking aide. Now, let us make haste, for the journey is a long one, and we must return home before nightfall."

They set off through a tunnel of dark trees. Thorn matched his steps to Morwid's, wondering what had prompted this visit to the village. The cave was well pro-visioned with everything they needed for their simple life beside the sea, and Morwid was not one to take unnecessary chances.

"What will we do in the village?" Thorn ventured when Morwid's long silence became too much to bear.

The old man muttered something and waved his hand, as if the answer to Thorn's question was of no importance.

"Will you tell us a story, then, to speed this journey along?"

At last the old man smiled, for there was little he liked better in the world than spinning tales. Some were true, some were not, and often Thorn could not tell which was which. But it hardly mattered, for Morwid's tales of battles were so vivid Thorn could imagine the thunderous charge of warhorses shaking the ground, the warriors' gleaming armor and flying pennants, and the horses' rearing at the clash of broadswords and poleaxes.

"Very well," Morwid said with obvious satisfaction. "A story. Long ago there were in these parts two kingdoms—Kelhadden and, across the river, Wyr. In most respects relations between the two were happy enough; people traveled freely from one to the other, and the two kings on more than one occasion had joined their armies to repel one invader or another."

"Like the Northmen?" Thorn stopped to remove a twig from the toe of his sandal, then hurried to catch up.

"Aye, though these events happened long before the Northmen came. But, to continue the tale, it happened that the king of Wyr had a daughter who was ugly as a toad, and though she had a pleasant singing voice and a dowry most generous, no appropriate match could be found for her."

"No suitable suitor!" Thorn crowed.

Morwid laughed. "Indeed. As the years went on, the king grew desperate to marry off his only child and so promised the entire kingdom of Wyr outright to whoever would pledge her his troth."

Sunlight had broken through the mist, warming the air. Morwid wiped his face with his sleeve and went on. "In Kelhadden there lived a poor knight, a cousin to King Warn's great-great-grandfather many times removed. Having no prospects, the knight sought out the king of Wyr and made a bargain to marry the princess. But as he was leaving the castle, he chanced upon a handmaiden gathering roses in the garden and was so smitten with her beauty he simply swept her onto his horse and made for the river, never to return."

"Then, he did not keep his promise to the king," Thorn said.

"And the entire kingdom paid the price. For the king of Wyr declared Kelhadden his mortal enemy and rode with his warriors across the river. A terrible battle ensued, in which thousands were killed. The stench of burning bodies hung in the air for weeks afterward."

The trail narrowed and the rooftops of the village appeared through the trees. Thorn strode along beside his teacher. "It was wrong of the king to kill thousands for the actions of one," he said, his upturned face serious. "And all because of his wounded pride."

"Aye. During the battle an amulet, which the king of Kelhadden wore around his neck, was broken and disappeared." Morwid's expression grew soft with remembering. "'Tis said it was a jewel whose radiance rivaled all others, though no one alive today can say precisely what it looked like."

"Surely the king could have gotten another amulet," Thorn said.

"If only it were that simple, our present troubles with the Northmen could have been avoided," Morwid said. "But the amulet was no ordinary thing. It was given to our first king by the spirits of sea, wind, and fire, and in it lies all power for good. But those same spirits have hidden it away until such time as there is a prince worthy of it. Kelhadden will not be safe from the likes of the Northmen till that prince finds it and brings it home."

"How will he find it if no one can describe it?" Thorn wondered aloud.

"Ah," Morwid said. "Here we are at last."

Thorn let out an exasperated sigh. He wanted an answer to his question, but Morwid always seemed to stop his tales just at the most interesting part. The old man quickened his steps, and they entered the village along a dusty road clogged with street beggars and sellers' stalls. Thorn's stomach clenched at the smells of ripe cheese, sausages, sweetmeats, and wine mixing with the sour stink of clogged cisterns and rotting cabbages in the street. He hastened to keep up with Morwid, who seemed quite intent upon a certain destination. They passed a deserted inn and the empty granary, which was overrun with hordes of screeching rats.

"By the saints!" Morwid muttered. "This village is a thousand times worse now than when I saw it last. Nobody has anything!"

"The Northmen stole every bit of grain," Thorn guessed.

"Aye, and long ago frightened away the lodgers at the inn. Ranulf's men have taken over the sellers' stalls too, though few there be who have any coins left to spend there. Kelhadden is bereft of almost everything save invaders and ghosts."

It was true. All along the streets, doors stood open as if people had simply stepped away on some quick errand, but peering into the grimy windows, Thorn could see tables and chairs layered with dust. A pall of unease hung over the entire village. Those who ventured into the streets darted about like frightened birds, quickly concluded their business with the Northmen, then hurried away without stopping to pass the time of day. Thorn searched the villagers' troubled faces, looking for answers to the questions that had troubled him since he was old enough to think of them: Who was he? Where were his parents? Why had they abandoned him to Morwid? A longing to know who he was and where he came from burned brightly in his chest.

At the far end of the street Morwid stopped suddenly and pointed to an abandoned merchant's cart lying near the crossroad. "Sit there and wait for me. And do not speak to anyone. I shan't be long."

Though he would have liked to explore, Thorn did as he was bidden. He perched on the cart, watching as Morwid glanced up and down the street before disappearing through a hastily opened door.

A ragged girl about Thorn's age ran past, her bare feet slapping on the cobblestones. Thorn, who for all his life had had no one save Morwid for company, longed to speak to her, but he dared not. Once or twice he had disobeyed Morwid and had paid dearly for his temerity. Conversation with the girl, however pleasant it might be, was not worth one of Morwid's lashings.

Soon Morwid returned clutching a small brown pouch and a bottle of amber-colored liquid. Thorn eyed the pouch. "Is there a sweet in there for me, Teacher?"

Morwid tucked the pouch away and said gruffly, "Step lively, boy. Time to go home."

Thorn crouched in the shadows and held himself still, his breathing slow and even. Wood smoke lay heavy in the air. Rotting leaves formed a spongy carpet beneath his feet. When the stag appeared, stepping silently through the mist, Thorn raised his bow and took aim. The arrow hissed, found its mark. The stag bolted, then fell.

Thorn unsheathed his skinning knife and crossed the clearing. Now a sturdy twelve-year-old, he was as strong as any man, yet he felt somehow half formed, as if a limb or an eye were missing. He felt certain the vague discontent that had plagued him all his life would evaporate as surely as mist over the sea if only he knew the answers to the questions that swirled constantly in his head. Was there somewhere in the forest, or beyond the sun-gilded sea, a mother and father who longed for him? A brother perhaps? Someone near his own age who would hear his secrets and laugh at his jokes?

He bent over the stag and slashed its belly. Blood and entrails rushed out. Steam rose off the warm carcass. When the animal had bled out, Thorn bound its legs with leather thongs, hoisted it over his shoulder, and started home.

A weak sun penetrated the fog, casting golden beams of light along the path. Above the still pond a cloud of silver moths hovered. Thorn noticed neither the weight of the stag, nor the beauty of the morning around him. Now his thoughts were of Morwid and the old man's mysterious book, a possession so cherished Thorn had never even been allowed to touch it. Only this morn, as Thorn prepared for the hunt, Morwid had sat before the fire, his shoulders hunched as if to protect the tome from the boy's prying eyes. And Thorn had wondered: Did the book contain the answers he needed? If only he knew how to read! But that was one skill Morwid had neglected to teach him.

Thorn reached the sea cave and found his mentor wearing leather leggings and the heavy cloak he favored from the first hint of winter's chill.

"Ah." Morwid returned his book to the stone ledge and eyed the stag with obvious satisfaction. "Well done. Leave it there and make haste. We have business at water's edge."

Thorn couldn't hide his surprise. Since a long illness last winter Morwid no longer traversed the trail down to the sea for fish; that was Thorn's job now.

"Forgive me, Teacher, but does that seem wise? The fog is thick this morn. The rocks will be slick as an eel."

The old warrior drew himself up. "Mayhap that is so, but time grows short and there is much to be done."

Much to be done. It was the old man's favored expression. Ever since Thorn could remember, he had been made to learn the arts of rope making and cliff climbing, been left to fend for himself at night in the darkness of the sea caves, and been sent to hunt game with aught but his budding bravery and a huntsman's bow. Under Morwid's patient eye he had learned the difference between poisonous mushrooms that would fell a man in an hour and the harmless ones that made a tasty meal after a long day in the woods. He learned to name the trees by their bark; now he knew the rough scales of the pin oak, the pale, bumpy skin of the birch. He was proud of his ability to track a stag, set a snare, and find his way home by reading the stars. He could brew potions for all manner of ailments and recite from memory the poetry of the ancients and the prayers of warriors long lost in the mists of time. Yet it seemed his education was not complete.

Morwid handed Thorn a length of rope the boy had only recently woven from reeds. "We shall go down the trail linked at the waist. Your sure steps will steady me."

Thorn's belly was empty. His muscles were stiff from carrying the stag up the steep trail. He had left the cave long before sunup in pursuit of game. What he wanted now was a bowl of warm broth and a long nap beside the fire. But Morwid's steadfast blue gaze brooked no argument. Resigned to his task, Thorn tied one end of the rope around his waist, then fastened the other end around Morwid's wiry middle. Down they went toward the sea, so slowly that the morn was nearly gone by the time they reached the water's edge.

Wisps of fog still hung above the sea and pressed onto the gray rocks. Waves hissed onto the sand. With his sleeve Morwid wiped his face, then untied the rope and let it fall. He clasped Thorn's shoulder. "I am well pleased with all you have learned. But there remains one thing more to master before you are ready."

"Before I am ready?" Thorn could not keep the impatience from his voice. "Since the day I took my first step, I have done all you asked of me though I don't understand why you set so many difficult tasks."

Morwid went on as if he hadn't heard. "Today you will swim."

At Thorn's quick intake of breath Morwid said, "We have neglected this lesson long enough. I cannot guess why you fear the water, but that matters not at all. You must overcome it."

Thorn himself could not explain the terror the sea held for him. From his earliest days he had delighted in running along the sand, collecting shells or bits of colored glass as gifts for Morwid. He loved the sight and smell of the sea, the sound of waves breaking on the rocks, and yet for as long as he could remember, the thought of the murky waves closing over his face terrified him.

Morwid shed his cloak and leggings and waded waist-deep into the water. "Come on in, boy."

The waves looked gray and angry. Fear rose in Thorn's chest, but he didn't want to displease the old man. Ofttimes Morwid had recited tales of his own brave exploits, tales that left no doubt as to his opinion of cowards. Thorn knew failure now might well condemn him to a lifetime of Morwid's contempt. Reluctantly he removed his leggings and, with a sense of dread, waded in up to his knees. The waves seemed to grow larger, pulsing and clawing at his tunic as he stood there, an arm's length from Morwid. His teacher held out his hand. "Do you not trust me?"

"It is this water I do not trust, Sir."

"Would I let you drown after all the trouble you have caused me these many years?"

"If I have been a burden, I beg your forgiveness." Thorn turned away, determined not to let Morwid see how deeply his words had stung.

"Watch me," Morwid commanded, taking Thorn's arm and turning him back around.

With that, the old man dove into the water. Only the back of his head showed above the curling ripples, and his hair spread across the surface like a long gray rope. Beneath the waves his feet moved like two small white fish. He swam a few strokes, then stood and motioned for Thorn to take his turn. "The secret is to become one with the water. Let it hold you up."

Though stiff with fright, Thorn took a breath and slid into the sea. The water closed over his head. His arms and legs flailed as the water took him. He felt blinded and bereft of speech. A dark fragment of memory pulled at him. Had he dreamed this moment, or had it actually happened before? Morwid's bony fingers clutched Thorn's waist. Thorn managed only one or two quick kicks before panic overcame pride and he sought the bottom with his feet and stood, shivering and gasping for breath.

A sudden breeze whipped the waves and chilled Thorn's skin. His teeth chattered. "Mayhap we should wait till I am older."

Morwid shook his head. "There is no time to waste. Try again."

Thorn lowered his face into the sea. Perhaps because he now knew what to expect, the rush of water filling his ears did not seem quite so terrifying. Dimly he could hear Morwid calling, "Kick!"

He kicked, holding his breath till his lungs seemed ready to burst. Instinctively he turned his head and gulped air. He felt himself moving through the waves. The tightness in his arms and legs loosened. But something was wrong. Morwid was no longer holding him up! He felt himself sinking into darkness. The waves closed over his head. His arms pinwheeled in the cold sea as his feet sought the ocean floor. At last he surfaced and spat a mouthful of salty water. "Help me!"

Morwid bobbed up beside Thorn. "There. That was not so difficult, eh?" He nodded toward the distant shore. "See how far you have come?"

Thorn suddenly felt weak and angry. "You promised not to let go!"

"I said I'd not let you drown. Enough for today. We shall practice again on the morrow."

"On the morrow I shall be dead from cold."

"I shall miss you very much," Morwid said gravely. "Now, swim ashore, boy. I should not like to walk the trail after dark."

Soon they were safely on land again. Thorn's fingers were stiff with cold as he sat on the wet ground tying his leggings. He blew on his hands to warm them, then refastened the rope around their waists. Morwid drew his woolen cloak tightly about his shoulders, and they made their slow way home.

By the time they had changed into dry clothes and spread their wet ones before the fire, darkness was falling. Thorn quickly butchered the stag. Morwid set some of the meat to roasting on the spit, while Thorn cut the rest into long strips for drying. The roasting meat sizzled and browned. Thorn's belly rumbled.

Morwid passed Thorn a slab of meat on a dented pewter plate. "Eat, then I have a story to tell."

Now that he was safe and dry, Thorn felt a secret surge of pride at having braved the sea. And next to a goodly supper and a warm fire, there was nothing he liked better than one of Morwid's stories. "Will you tell a tale of the Northmen?" he asked between bites.

"Aye. The Northmen have a part in this tale. 'Tis a long one, and quite unpleasant, for it is the story of the terrible things that befell Kelhadden long before you were born. But it is time you heard it." Morwid wiped his hands on his tunic. From its hiding place on the stony ledge he extracted his book and brought it back to the fire. He waved his hand as if making an introduction. "The Book of Ancients, which has guided our kingdom since the beginning of time."

So here was Morwid's book at last! Fascinated, Thorn took it and ran his fingers over thin, faded pages that smelled of dust and leather and something secret he could not name. Though he had never before touched it, the book somehow seemed comforting and familiar. His heart beat strangely in his chest. Perhaps now Morwid would teach him to read. Then he would see whether this book could tell him what he wished to know.

"Long ago," Morwid began, "there lived in Kelhadden a king called Warn."

"I know that," Thorn said. "You were his chief warrior and his counselor."

"Aye. Kelhadden was a pleasant kingdom then. The king was generous to his subjects, and they fared well in their shops and fields. The village was a bustling place of inns and taverns and shops. On market days the streets rang with the voices of tanners and ribbon sellers and horse traders, all hawking their wares. There were mimes and bards and jesters aplenty. King

Warn often invited them to the castle for days of merry-making."

"But then Ranulf and the Northmen came and defeated the king," Thorn supplied, wishing Morwid would hurry along to the new part of the tale.

"It was not so simple as that, young one." Taking the book from Thorn, Morwid said, "In this book lies the wisdom of the ancients, the promises and warnings of seers and prophets. Even kings ignore it at their peril."

Morwid turned the pages carefully until he found the one he sought. He tipped the book toward the firelight and read aloud: "'In the ninth year of the ninth king the kingdom will be besieged. Cunning and patience must prevail over vanity and pride.'" He looked up. "Warn was the ninth king, after the death of his cousin Galos. It was just after Michaelmas some fifteen years ago that Ranulf and his Northmen came. First by ship, then by foot along the road by the sea, and then to a camp on the far side of the river. A hunting party discovered them there and came at once to the castle to tell the king."

The fire was burning low. Thorn got up to add more wood. Morwid waited till the boy was seated again before continuing. "We devised a battle plan to repel the invaders. I advised Warn that we bide our time and wait for the Northmen to cross the river. Then my men and I would engage them in battle, whilst another party closed in behind them and blocked their escape. But after a fortnight the Northmen still had not moved, and people in the kingdom grew impatient. Some said the king was afraid. Some said he was too weak to protect them." Morwid shook his head. "Against my counsel and the warnings of the ancients, King Warn, to prove his bravery, summoned his warriors and rode out to the river."

"You as well?" Thorn asked.

"Against my better judgment, aye. For I had sworn fealty to my sovereign and was duty-bound to obey him. Of course, without the amulet to protect us, we were overrun in a trice. Besides King Warn, just two others and I survived the rout and were taken to the dungeon in chains." Morwid's features hardened at the memory. "A terrible place that was, all cold stone and dark shadows. To this day it haunts my dreams. Ranulf stood upon the throne and proclaimed himself king, and there he has remained from that day to this."

"How did you escape the dungeon?"

A sad smile crossed Morwid's wrinkled face. "King Warn had a daughter, a beautiful girl she was. And scarcely older than you at the time. For days after our capture Isotta begged Ranulf's leave to bring us some ale and bread, and at last he agreed. She brought us food and the key to our chains, concealed beneath her cloak. But before we could make good our escape,

Ranulf discovered her deception and offered her a bargain. He would allow us to leave Kelhadden unharmed if she agreed to marry him. We bade her not to accept, for any of us would rather have died in our chains than have her wed such an odious man. But she agreed in order to spare her father a life in the dungeon."

Thorn marveled at Isotta's courage. He couldn't imagine how anyone could be so brave. "She sacrificed her own happiness for that of another."

"True nobility often requires sacrifice," Morwid said. He went on. "Of course, Ranulf did not keep his word. The day after the nuptials he released us, only to send his henchmen to ambush us on the road. One of our party was recaptured and returned to the dungeon. Two others, including the king, were beheaded. I escaped with nothing but the clothes on my back and this book, hidden beneath my tunic."

Thorn frowned. "The people should have taken back Kelhadden."

"Oh, you may be sure 'tis not from lack of trying. As soon as I could, I gathered every able-bodied man twixt here and the summer country to fight against the Northmen. But it was useless, for the invaders had taken our horses and weapons, and all the provisions in our fields and storehouses. There was neither dirk nor spear, nor bread nor meat, to be had at any price." Morwid paused, remembering. "After a time Ranulf realized he could enrich himself even more by forcing our people into labor. Most fled to the forest rather than submit, but a few villagers decided to stay and make the best of it. Now, of course, the Northmen sell them just enough food to keep them alive and toiling in the fields. You saw it for yourself some years ago, and since then things have only become worse. Even the church bells have gone silent. And those who oppose Ranulf still live in hiding."

"The forest people," Thorn said.

"Aye. They are the last of those who once were the flesh and bone of our kingdom. They have lost everything, except the hope that someday their prince will appear and reclaim Kelhadden, just as the ancients have foretold."

"But the prince must find the lost amulet first," Thorn said, remembering Morwid's long-ago story. "And that seems impossible."

"Difficult, but not impossible for a prince who has mastered the proper skills." Morwid grasped Thorn's arm with more strength than Thorn supposed the old man possessed. "And that is the reason for the tasks I have set for you, Thorn."

Inside the firelit cave Morwid's voice fell to a whisper. "You are that prince."

CHAPTER THREE

THORN'S LAUGHTER ECHOED INSIDE THE DIM CAVE. "By my troth, Sir, that is the most fanciful tale you have ever told."

But Morwid was not smiling. "I am glad it amuses you, but every word I have spoken is the truth." He gnawed on a joint of meat and tossed the bone away. "You will make a journey to places yet unknown, and there you will find the amulet."

To hide his confusion, Thorn turned away and took his time adding more twigs to the fire. Nothing had prepared him for such news. He was neither as brave and smart as Morwid, nor as strong and cunning as Ranulf and the Northmen. At last he said, "I am honored you think me worthy of it, but even if I were the prince, I would have no wish to claim the kingdom."

Morwid said nothing.

Dismayed at the burden suddenly thrust upon him, Thorn cried, "How can this be? You have told me a thousand times of the day you found me here, thrown away like yesterday's ash. A true prince would be treasured and cosseted, not cast aside like rubble."

"I cannot explain everything," Morwid said with an exasperated sigh. "I know only what the Book of Ancients decrees."

"Mayhap that book of yours holds no more truth than the fairy stories you told me when I was a babe."

Morwid clutched the tome to his chest as if it were a living thing capable of being wounded by Thorn's sharp words. "In all my life it has never been wrong. Like it or not, you are the one fate has chosen."

"How can you know that?" Thorn cried.

Opening the book again, Morwid said, "Listen to this secret, known to only me and those with whom I have chosen to share it. 'Golden hair and golden eye, such are signs to know him by.' Does that not describe you exactly?"

Thorn shrugged. "There must be hundreds of boys with hair like mine. Among the Northmen alone are many whose hair is the color of wheat."

"True enough, but I have never seen another

golden-eyed boy, not even among the Northmen." Morwid set his book aside. "I will admit there were times when I wondered whether you were the promised one. But never have I known any boy to so quickly master the ways of the wood and the secrets of the stars. More than once I have thought you must indeed be touched by magic."

Those words gave Thorn pause, for there were times when he, too, was at a loss to explain how he knew just where to find the tastiest mushrooms or the fattest hare, and just where to place his feet on the rocky cliffs to avoid falling to his death. He remembered one foggy night when he'd become hopelessly lost on the sea cliffs, with no inkling of which way led home. But somehow his vision had pierced the darkness, and as if magically guided by an unseen hand, he had followed the stars home.

Morwid continued. "I am but an old man, full of hope that has made me rash. Perhaps I should not have given you the news this way, but time grows short. Our people cannot last much longer."

Thorn pushed his plate away, his hunger gone in the wake of this unsettling news. Though he had never spoken of it, he had of late begun to dream of the day he would leave Morwid's cave and go out into the world on his own. He thought he might become a renowned huntsman or perhaps a traveling musician, for he had grown quite skillful with his flute. He could become a soldier in some far-off kingdom or learn to captain a great ship. He could imagine standing at the wheel of his own sleek vessel, the salt spray coating his lips, the sails billowing and the pennants flying as he raced to the very edge of the world. Now all his secret dreams were dashed like flotsam upon jagged rocks.

"Come." Morwid returned the book to its place on the ledge and picked up his staff and cloak. "Fill my pouch with some of that meat and follow me."

"Now? In the dead of night?"

"Darkness will hide us from Ranulf's men, if they be hereabouts."

Thorn swallowed the bitterness rising in his throat. Since waking this morn he had felled the stag, led Morwid down the steep cliff, braved the cold sea just to please the old man, and led him home again. He had prepared the meat for drying and listened patiently to Morwid's preposterous tale. All he wanted now was to be left alone to sort out the disappointment and confusion roiling inside him. But he donned his cloak and followed Morwid into the night.

They took a long-abandoned path leading away from the cave. The full moon shone bright as torchlight as they descended into the trees, past a brackish pond teeming with insects, past a cluster of abandoned huts with caved-in roofs and broken chimneys. Beside a crumbling stone fence Morwid halted and gestured with his staff toward a stand of apple trees. "This was once the finest orchard in the entire kingdom," he said quietly, "but Ranulf burned it lest the people gain some use of it."

As he spoke, Morwid broke off a handful of twigs and tossed them onto a blackened stump protruding through a gap in the fence. He leaned on his staff for a moment longer, then turned abruptly and brushed his fingers against his cloak. "Come along, boy."

He motioned to Thorn, and they continued along the trail till they reached the deepest part of the forest, where the faint path abruptly ended. Now the trees were so dense no moonlight entered. Thorn could scarcely see his hand before his face, but Morwid's steps were sure as the man and boy moved soundlessly through the undergrowth. The forest was eerily silent, as if all life had been stolen from it. Tangled vines curled about Thorn's ankles as he hurried after Morwid. The air grew thick with the familiar, sooty smell of a wood fire and with other, strange odors Thorn could not name. Despair settled around him like a gray fog. Even if he were the prince, he could never erase the pain and suffering, the heavy cloak of hopelessness pressing down around him. He wanted to go home.

"There," Morwid whispered at last. Peering through the darkness, Thorn could see a flickering light shining in the distance and the faint outline of a tiny hut nestled like a mushroom in the undergrowth. Morwid nudged Thorn forward. "Hurry, hurry. There is much to be done before daylight comes."

When they arrived, Morwid knocked three times, waited, then knocked again. The door opened and there stood a gray-haired woman in blue robes holding a sputtering candle. "Come in," she said quietly, and ushered them inside.

Thorn looked around. Near the fire a small table held a ball of amber glass, a vessel of water, and a forest of stubby, unlit candles. On a shelf beneath the cobwebbed window sat a woven basket overflowing with feathers of black, blue, and bright green. Nearby lay a carving knife with a curved handle, and several bits of smooth white bone.

The woman placed a hand on Thorn's shoulder. "You were scarcely four years old the last time I saw you, and on your way to the village with Morwid. I am Drucilla."

Morwid set down his staff. "When he was born, you said to bring him back when he was twelve, and here he is."

"And you still want to know whether he is the prince."

"Now I believe he is indeed the one the Book of Ancients promised," Morwid said. "'Tis the boy himself who needs convincing." He plopped down on a stool beside the fire.

"Is this true, Thorn?" Drucilla asked.

Thorn's head swam with more questions than he could possibly ask. He nodded and finally managed to add, "If I am the prince, how will I ever find the amulet? No one knows—"

"Where it is or what it looks like," the seer finished. "I'm afraid my gift has faded over the years, but I'll do what I can. Come. Sit here."

Thorn sat. Drucilla placed her hand on Thorn's chest, squarely over his heart, and closed her eyes. The tiny hut soon filled with a humming sound that reminded Thorn of swarming bees. He could feel the vibration of her fingers against his skin, a sensation that was unsettling but not painful.

The humming grew louder. Drucilla's arm, then her whole body, began to shake. Tears formed at the corners of her eyes and fell onto her blue robe. She withdrew her hand. The humming stopped. Then the seer stepped back and made a deep curtsy. "My prince."

"Aha!" Morwid exclaimed with the excited glee of one who had discovered buried treasure. "I knew it! What did I tell you, Thorn? The Book of Ancients is never wrong."

Thorn sat there stunned. He could not say why he believed the old woman. He knew only that somehow her touch had changed him, had removed his doubts. "I am the prince of Kelhadden," he said in a voice tinged with wonder. "But I still don't know the reason I am a secret prince, or where to find the amulet, or—"

"One question at a time, if it please you, Sir," Drucilla said. "I am old as dirt and not as strong as I once was."

"But you will help me?"

"If only I were younger," Drucilla said. "Fifty years ago I could have looked into my scrying glass and told you exactly where to find the amulet, but alas, I am winding down like a worn-out timepiece, and there is little I can offer you now."

"Drucilla," Morwid interjected. "When Thorn was a babe, you said something I have wondered about all these years."

"I remember. 'One alone, then two as one, until at last the quest be done.'"

"What does it mean?" Morwid asked.

Drucilla shrugged. "I cannot say for certain. I know only that when I read Thorn's chest just now, I felt the power of two hearts, just as I saw them in the scrying glass twelve years ago. Perhaps it means he will find someone to help him in his quest. On the other hand, it may mean he will encounter a powerful enemy who wishes to possess the amulet for his own purposes." She fixed her gaze upon the young prince. "Be ever on your guard, Sir. We *must* have our amulet back, before it is too late."

So saying, Drucilla opened a wooden cask and took out a leather pouch filled with sharp-smelling herbs. "In my scrying glass this morn I saw that you were coming today. Hoping you were indeed the prince, I mixed a dream potion to aid you in your quest."

Thorn sniffed the pouch and wrinkled his nose. "What is it made of?"

"That does not matter. You must go to the summer country, for that is the place the spirits of water, fire, and earth favor when they wish to conceal something of great importance. Once you are there, make a brew with rainwater, and sleep. In your dreams you will learn where the amulet is hidden."

"Suppose I do not dream?" Thorn asked. "What shall I do then?"

Drucilla smiled. "'Tis unwise to borrow trouble, if you will forgive my saying so."

Morwid rose and took up his staff. He kissed the seer's cheek. "We must go. There is still much to be done. Soon our dreams for the kingdom will come to pass."

"Wait," Drucilla said. "Though I am not of much use in finding the amulet, perhaps there is something I can do to help." She bustled to the table and mixed some green and blue herbs with a cup of water from her kettle. She lit her candles and closed her eyes. Then, holding her fingers lightly above the cup, she softly chanted, "Boil and bubble, mystic charm, keep this prince from mortal harm."

She handed it to Thorn. "Drink this, my prince, and may all the spirits of heaven and earth aid you in your quest."

Thorn drank the concoction, which reminded him of the wild mint tea Morwid often brewed when cold winds raked the sea cliffs. He set the empty cup on the table and picked up his heavy pouch.

Drucilla opened the door and looked out. "All is quiet, but do be careful, Sir."

Thorn thanked the seer, and just like that, he and Morwid were again walking in the deep forest. Too stunned by the night's events to speak, Thorn merely followed Morwid as they wound through the undergrowth. After they had walked for some minutes, Morwid paused and pointed to a pinprick of light in the darkness.

"There be the last of the forest people," he said quietly, "struggling to survive till their prince can rescue them. Take care not to show yourself."

They edged closer to the flickering fire until Thorn could see the ravaged faces of old men, several women, and a knot of children in threadbare cloaks, huddled silently near the flames. Two boys about his own age, thin and barefoot, shared the remnants of a blanket. Thorn thought of evenings at his own fireside when the sea cave rang with the sounds of Morwid's merry tales or some lively tune played upon his flute. "They do not speak?" he whispered.

"Hunger and fear have stolen their tongues. They once begged for the skin and bones of hares from Ranulf's huntsmen, but now even that is denied them. Many have died of a dozen afflictions of body and mind, with aught to ease their pain." Morwid leaned heavily upon his staff. "For years I brought them healing herbs and food as often as I could, but now I am too old to be of much use. They dare not show themselves while Ranulf rules, and they will not last another winter in this wood."

"Ranulf will not rest till they all are dead and no one is left to challenge him," Thorn said, surprised at the intensity of his own feelings. "As if a few children and old men pose any threat to him!"

Thorn felt Morwid's smile in the dark. "Ah. You feel the weight of this great injustice at last."

One of the women rose and left the circle of light. An old man, leaning on a makeshift walking cane, stood to tend the fire, and Thorn saw there was nothing but a stump where his right foot belonged.

"That is Golwyn," Morwid murmured. "Once a scholar and the king's best mapmaker. It was he who was taken back to the castle in chains after Ranulf pretended to release us. He lost his foot to Ranulf's poleax for refusing to turn over his map of the summer country. It was said in Kelhadden that Ranulf then staked him in the sun and left him to the vultures. He nearly died from it."

So much misery born of Ranulf's callous greed! Thorn clenched his fists and swallowed the revulsion and anger welling up inside him.

Morwid went on in his whispery voice, "Next to Golwyn sits Gareth, who was away the day Ranulf came to Kelhadden. Of course he was arrested the moment he returned. He managed to escape only by great good luck. But I do not see Gareth's brother Marcus." He sighed. "I fear death has taken him."

"Will you speak to them?" Thorn asked. "I should think the sight of such a loyal friend as you would cheer them."

"And it would cheer me to greet them," Morwid said. "But if Ranulf or his men should see us together, it would put them in further danger. I won't risk it."

Abruptly he tapped Thorn's pouch. "Continue along this line of trees till you are past the campfire. Near their huts you will find three stumps clustered together. Leave the meat there, then come back quickly. And watch for Ranulf's men."

"But—"

"Hurry!" Morwid said. "The darkness wanes, and we must be away."

Thorn moved quietly along the forest floor, edging past the miserable little band huddled before the fire, till he found the makeshift shelters and the three stumps. He crouched in the shadows and left the meat in the hollow of the tallest one. As he rose, a stone whizzed past his head. He ducked, and the stone landed in the bushes behind him. He stood still, his heart thumping against his chest. Suppose Ranulf's men had discovered him? Suppose they had stumbled across Morwid hiding in the trees? Footsteps came steadily onward in the dark. Thorn clutched his empty pouch, trying to decide whether to speak, run, or remain silent.

"Oh!" A woman emerged from the trees and dropped her handful of stones right in front of Thorn. So far removed from the circle of firelight, he could see nothing of her face, only a wisp of hair springing from the hood of her cloak, and her small white hands now clasped tightly to her chest. He felt, rather than saw, her searching gaze. She spoke not another word but briefly touched his arm before disappearing into the shadows.

The skin on Thorn's arm warmed and tingled, much as it had when Drucilla had touched him. His head swam with the strange alchemy in the cloaked woman's touch. For a moment he thought he knew her somehow, and she knew him, that somewhere he had seen her before. But of course that was impossible.

Walking as fast as he dared, he retraced his steps and found Morwid waiting near the path.

"Thorn?" Morwid muttered.

"Aye."

The old warrior grunted and stood. Thorn handed him the empty leather pouch. Morwid retrieved his staff, and they started home.

Something in the ruined orchard rustled as they passed. Thorn whirled, all his senses suddenly alert. He started to speak, but Morwid silenced him with a quick shake of his head and pushed Thorn ahead of him up the darkened trail.

As they neared their cave, a bright moon appeared, casting a silver path far out on the dark water, illuminating the ghostly shapes of the rocks along the shore and revealing the empty path in front of them. Thorn felt the tension leave his shoulders.

When Morwid stopped to regain his breath, Thorn leaned against a mossy outcropping and said, "May I speak freely, Teacher?"

Morwid snorted. "You always speak freely, even when it would be wiser to listen. But go ahead. Speak, if you will."

"'Tis clear to me now that it is my duty to banish Ranulf from Kelhadden. The whole way up this cliff I have pondered how best to do it, once I have found the amulet, but there are no answers, only more questions."

Morwid was quiet for so long Thorn thought the old man had fallen asleep. But presently he spoke. "No one can make muddy water run clear, but if you allow it to remain still, it will eventually clear itself." Gesturing to the rocks below and the dark sea washing over them, he continued, "Be patient and you will see your way."

Without warning, three hulking forms suddenly materialized on the trail in front of them. In the moonlight Thorn could see the gleam of their weapons and the straw-colored hair that marked them as Northmen. The tallest one wore a bushy beard and a sweeping cloak shot through with shimmering threads. "Morwid!" he bellowed. "I prayed the fates would one day send you into my path, and by the saints, they have done it!"

"'Tis Ranulf!" Morwid cried. "Run, Thorn!"

But Thorn stood rooted to the spot, staring up at a man of soaring height, thick as a column of stone, with granite-hard, hate-filled eyes. For a moment neither boy nor man moved. Then Ranulf shouted to one of his men, "Olfar! There is Morwid at last. Take him!"

Morwid raised his staff as Olfar grabbed him and shoved him to his knees. The staff skittered over the stones.

"Morwid!" Thorn yelled. Almost without thinking,

he hefted a rock, aimed squarely at Olfar's head, and heaved it with all his might. The man bellowed, clutched his head, and staggered. Before he could recover, Thorn threw himself at Olfar's knees and sent him toppling off the cliff. He heard the scrape of the Northman's boots and the ring of his sword on stone as the man clung to a ledge below.

Morwid moaned and tried to rise, but before Thorn could help him, the other Northman grabbed the boy from behind.

"Let me go!" Thorn yelled. He kicked with all his might and elbowed his captor, but Trevyn held him fast. "What shall I do with this wild upstart, Your Majesty?" he shouted. "By my bones, he's strong as an ox."

Before Ranulf could reply, Olfar's voice echoed through the trees. "Trevyn!" he shouted to his companion. "Help me!"

The one called Trevyn shoved Thorn aside and rushed to the ledge, shouting to Olfar, "Hold on while I get my rope."

Thorn wheeled and saw that Ranulf had drawn his sword and was aiming it straight for Morwid's heart. Thorn frantically sought another stone. Instead his fingers closed over Morwid's staff, lying across the path. He snatched it up and cracked it sharply across Ranulf's shins just as the sword came down. With a piercing cry, Morwid crumpled onto the dirt.

"Morwid!" Thorn cried.

"He cannot help you now," Ranulf said, wincing and rubbing his shins.

"You had no right to harm him!" Thorn cried. "Can you not see he is old and only half your size?"

A massive fist crashed into the side of Thorn's face and sent him tumbling backward into the dirt. Ranulf towered over him. "Watch your tongue, cretin. Who do you think you are, speaking to your king in such a manner?"

Thorn began to tremble. Pain shot through his jaw and shoulder. He could hear Morwid's groans and the voices of the two men on the ledge. Ranulf grabbed Thorn's tunic and hauled him roughly to his feet.

"Well?" the Northman growled. "Have you suddenly gone mute, boy? When I ask a question, I expect an answer!"

Thorn was too terrified to speak and ashamed of his cowardice. He could do nothing but stare at the arrogant giant looming over him.

Ranulf raised his fist again. Cold with panic, Thorn twisted free and sidestepped the blow. To his astonishment, great gales of laughter burst from the Northman. Arms akimbo, he rocked forward, then tipped his head back and laughed until his entire frame shook.

"Look at you!" Ranulf said at last. "You shrink from a blow like a stinking cur."

Thorn said nothing. He trembled with rage. *Thief,* he thought. *Murderer. I hate him!*

Trevyn rushed to Ranulf's side. "Quickly, Sir, if you will. Olfar clings to life on the ledge. I have tried to rescue him with my rope, but he is so heavy I can't pull him up." Trevyn glanced at Morwid, lying motionless on the ground. "Leave him there. He is old and weak. If he lives until sunrise, the vultures will make short work of him."

Ranulf laughed again, a harsh, disagreeable sound. "Good riddance." Without warning, he savagely boxed both Thorn's ears. "Be glad I have someone far more important to attend to, my little coward, or I would teach you a hard lesson indeed. Go now, before I put you in chains for your impudence." Then he strode toward the ledge with Trevyn.

Thorn crouched in the shadows and shook his head to clear the ringing in his ears. He wanted to tend Morwid, but he dared not move until Ranulf and Trevyn had rescued their companion and moved off down the trail. When they had gone, he rushed to Morwid's side. "Teacher?"

"Home," Morwid whispered. "Help me up."

It was then Thorn realized he was kneeling in a sticky pool of Morwid's blood. He felt like crying, but there was no time for tears.

"We cannot go home just yet," he said. "You are too

badly hurt. I will get your potions from the cave and come back right away."

"No time. We will go now." Morwid sat up, clutching his chest.

Stubborn old goat, Thorn thought in an unbidden rush of love for the old warrior. Whatever his faults, Morwid did not deserve this wound. But such cruelty would go on unchecked so long as the Northmen held the kingdom. A deep desire for justice took root in Thorn's bones. To hide his churning emotions, he said, "When I am king, Sir, you *will* obey me."

He bent his knees and hoisted Morwid onto his shoulder, surprised to find the old man weighed less than the stag he had killed—was it only this morn? With a start he realized the entire night had passed. In the light of a new dawn he pushed steadily up the trail till they were home.

Inside the cave he removed Morwid's cloak to expose the ragged wound in his chest. "At least Ranulf missed your heart," he said, his voice shaking.

"My pouch . . . deflected the blow."

Thorn cleaned Morwid's wound and began tearing strips of his own cloak to bind it.

"The cautery iron," Morwid rasped.

Only once, after Morwid had been wounded by an angry she-bear, had Thorn seen his teacher use the iron to scorch his own wounded flesh. Thorn still remembered

Morwid's scream as the rod made contact with his skin, and the sickly sweet stench that lingered in the cave afterward. Now he said to his mentor, "I cannot."

"You must . . . stop the bleeding. Get it."

Reluctantly Thorn took the long-handled rod from the shelf and set it in the fire. While it heated, he filled a water pot, opened jars of balsam leaves and balm, and finished tearing strips for a bandage. When the iron glowed red, he spat on it, and it hissed.

"I am ready," Morwid said.

Thorn's eyes blurred as he lifted the iron and pressed it against Morwid's gaping wound. The flesh sizzled, blackened.

Morwid's body stiffened. He cried out once, a long, animal-like howl, then grew still. Thorn waved the balsam leaves beneath Morwid's nose, applied balm to the wound, and bandaged it as quickly as he could. Then he boiled some comfrey, sweetened it with honey, and helped Morwid sip it. Soon the ravaged warrior drifted into sleep. Thorn wrapped himself in his blanket and hovered nearby, anxiously watching the slow rise and fall of Morwid's chest.

The wind came up, buffeting the trees. Somewhere out over the sea, thunder rumbled. Rain stuttered on the rocks. Thorn felt bone tired, but his head was full of questions. He was the prince. Then, was Ranulf his father? If so, would not the fierce

Northman have recognized his own son? Why had his mother left him in this cave with Morwid? Most worrisome of all was the question of the king's lost amulet. How would he find it when no one could describe it?

Morwid grunted. Instantly Thorn threw off his blanket and shot to his feet, but the old man said, "Quiet your mind and rest. The sun is nearly up and soon you must be away."

Thorn fell into a short and fitful sleep, then woke with a start. The fire was almost out; the air inside the cave smelled of balm and charred flesh. He rose to rekindle the fire, surprised to find Morwid already awake and moving gingerly about the cave.

"You must go . . . quickly, Thorn," he said, "before Ranulf changes his mind and returns to look for you." His old eyes were watery and red rimmed, whether from the pain of his wound or sadness at their parting Thorn could not say.

Thorn peered out of the cave. The rain had slackened to a heavy mist. Under a leaden sky the wind nudged the waves onto the rocks. "'Tis not much of a day for beginning a journey." He tried to keep his tone light, but a hard knot throbbed painfully in his throat.

"Behind that gray stone just above the entrance you will find a wooden cask," Morwid said. "Bring it to me." Thorn complied. Morwid opened the lid and spread its contents on the floor. "Here are the tools you will need for your quest," he said with a wave of his hand, "just as the ancients have ordained." He handed Thorn an ebony-handled dirk. "Your weapon. Guard it well."

Thorn inspected the knife. Though the handle was long and smooth, the blade finely wrought and perfectly balanced, Thorn wondered whether a sharp lance or a sturdy sword might be more useful. And the other things Morwid set before him—a mirror, a ball of twine, a single arrow, a bowl, and a broken seashell—were so ordinary they seemed unnecessary for this journey.

As if reading Thorn's thoughts, Morwid gestured toward the items lying on the ground. "You are wondering about these things. The bowl is made of earth, the blade of your knife tempered by fire. The shell will serve as your water cup, the arrow as a wand of the air. Earth and fire, water and wind . . . shall be your enemies . . . and your servants."

To his growing bundle Thorn added his blanket, his bow, and a quiver of arrows. Then some venison, salted fish, dried berries, and packets of rosemary, sage, and comfrey.

Morwid removed from around his own neck a leather cord, at the end of which was suspended a moonstone, round and smooth as a pearl. "When you are king . . . you must choose a counselor. Give him this stone as a symbol of the trust between you . . . as it was given to me by King Warn. Choose well, boy, for a wise counselor is a prize beyond price."

Thorn slipped the moonstone over his head and tucked it inside his tunic. Then from his cask Morwid produced a square of leather, upon which was drawn a map. With one bony finger he traced a route. "Here lies our cave, and there, the village at Kelhadden. Follow the river road for some days until you reach the summer country. Have you the potion Drucilla made for you?"

"Aye."

"Brew it as she has instructed, and then you will dream. Now, let me look at you."

Thorn stood there, a tall, strong-shouldered boy in a blood-spattered tunic and a tattered cloak. Weighted with his quiver and bow, and his many provisions, he thought surely he must look more like a peddler than a prince.

Resting his hand on Thorn's shoulder, Morwid said, "Your fate has arrived just as the heavens foretold. Go now . . . and meet it with courage."

"Be well, Teacher." A rush of words crowded Thorn's mind, words of gratitude for all Morwid had taught him, expressions of regret for all the ways he had surely disappointed the old warrior, fears and uncertainties about the long journey that lay ahead. But he spoke none of them; Morwid expected him to be strong, to embrace his destiny with bravery and grace.

Instead he said, "When I find the amulet, I will come for you, and we will go to the castle together, for the victory shall be yours as much as mine."

"No!" Morwid said, so forcefully that Thorn jumped. "Do not come back here. I will meet you . . . on the road to the castle and return to Kelhadden as I left it, with the Book of Ancients under my cloak."

Now there could be no more delay. Thorn did not trust himself to speak. His throat ached with tears, but it would not do to shed them.

Morwid turned his back and busied himself with his bottles and potions. "Go."

CHAPTER FOUR

A SEA BREEZE SHOOK THE LAST RAIN FROM THE TREES. The pale sun lit the path through the forest. In the calm afternoon light the deep wood did not seem quite so forbidding. Now that he was on his way at last, Thorn felt almost lighthearted, for in finding the king's lost amulet, he thought he might learn the answers to his questions about himself. He kept up a brisk pace, stopping only once to drink from the stream. On silent huntsman's feet he passed the rotted tree stumps where he had seen the forest woman, half hoping for another encounter. He couldn't shake the feeling that somehow they were connected, though reason told him it was impossible. Nearby the bushes rustled. Thorn halted, imagining dozens of pairs of eyes watching his progress through the tangled undergrowth, but nothing moved and he went on.

Farther into the depths of the forest the trail began a steep ascent. Here and there ferns protruded from moss-furred ledges jutting into the path. The ground grew hard and slick, slowing his progress, so that it was late in the day when Thorn reached the crest of the hill and stopped to get his bearings.

The light was fading; already the valley floor lay in shadow. To his left stood Kelhadden's gray stone church with its arched windows and silent belfry; to his right, a cluster of sturdy thatch-roofed houses now occupied by the Northmen. In the lane above the meadow one of Ranulf's shepherds drove his stolen flock. Thorn turned and looked in the other direction. The winding trail to Morwid's sea cave was lost from view, but on the horizon rose the castle at Kelhadden. As he watched, the first lanterns winked on in the distant windows, shining like gold coins in the dusk. Thorn tried to imagine himself living there among artful tapestries and gleaming silver. He wondered what it would feel like to sleep on a soft bed and have sweets to eat anytime he wanted.

He marveled at how quickly his life had changed. Only days ago his future had seemed rich with any number of possibilities; now there was only one path open to him: to find the amulet and claim Kelhadden.

The breeze cooled his skin. His stomach groaned. Leaving the trail, he walked a short distance into the woods, where he took shelter beneath a canopy of trees. Thorn opened his pack and ate some of the salted fish and a handful of the dried berries Morwid had provided, then wrapped himself in his cloak. Though he was weary after his day on the trail, he could not rest; the presence of the Northmen in the valley below was too troubling. He lay on the ground, all his senses amplified. Leaves rustled in the stillness. In the undergrowth the night birds called and fluttered. Once, Thorn thought he heard footsteps on the trail, and he reached for his dirk. When his ears grew strained with listening and no one appeared, he lay on his back, naming the stars one by one until he fell into an uneasy sleep.

In the morning he ate quickly and started off again. The trail leveled out, and he walked steadily all morning till the path ended and he came to the road Morwid had promised. Soon after midday he stopped beside a small waterfall to rest. He washed the dust from his face and climbed onto a boulder to take a look around. Shading his eyes, he scanned the horizon, but the sea cave, the forest, and the castle were far behind him now. Through the sun-spattered leaves he saw in the distance the broad gray snake of a river wending its way to the summer country and on toward the sea.

"Show me your hands!" said a voice so suddenly that Thorn lost his balance and toppled off the boulder, cracking his elbow on the stones below.

He reached for his dirk. "Who goes there?"

"I shall ask the questions and you will answer!"

Thorn scanned the undergrowth for the source of the imperious voice, but he could see nothing.

"Up here, you lubber!"

Thump. An acorn landed squarely on Thorn's head. He looked up. In the oak above him sat a boy about his own age. The boy flashed a grin and shinnied down to the lowest branch, where he hung motionless for a moment before dropping to the ground. He was thin and dark, and dressed in a saffron cap topped off by a gleaming raven's feather. His moss green cape was fastened at the throat with a bit of carved bone. A huntsman's bow and a silver flute protruded from his leather pack.

Thorn had never seen anyone like this strange boy, who was clearly not a Northman.

"How did you do that?" Thorn asked. "I could not tell from which direction your voice came."

"That is my secret. If you don't mind, put that dirk away before someone gets hurt. Had I meant to harm you, I had but to drop a stone upon your head. Now, pray tell, what brings you here?"

"That is *my* secret!" Thorn retorted.

"Hmmm. Since you are upon this road with Kelhadden at your back, I suppose you are on your way to the summer country."

Thorn remembered Drucilla's warning: There may be another who seeks the amulet. He said, "I cannot say where I will go. I am off on an adventure."

"Splendid! Methinks I will join you, for I could use a change of scenery." The boy bowed to Thorn. "I am called Galystawen, but if that be too much for your tongue to master, a simple Raven will do. In fact, I prefer it."

Charmed despite himself, Thorn smiled. "Raven suits you," he said. "I am called Thorn."

"A goodly name for one of such sharp tongue, and even sharper wits. What say we continue along this road till this day is done. If we prove agreeable companions, there will be time on the morrow to choose a destination."

Thorn considered this. It might be days before he came to the end of this road. A companion would surely make the journey seem shorter. Still, he wasn't sure he should risk it. Suppose Raven *were* his enemy?

"Come, come." Raven shot Thorn another disarming grin. "I assure you, I am completely trustworthy. Let us be off!" He took out his flute and fashioned an enchanting tune. "To adventure! And may the fates grant us safe journey."

Vowing silently to keep a close watch on his odd companion, Thorn shouldered his pack, and the boys set off, walking side by side. After they had gone some distance, Raven said, "Every man has a story. Tell me yours."

"I am an orphan," Thorn said easily, stopping to shake a pebble from his boot. "Reared in a cave by a wise old man who taught me all I know."

"Reared in a cave?" Raven laughed. "Oh, this is indeed a promising beginning, for there is nothing I enjoy more than the company of a teller of tales. If it please you, tell me more."

"It is not so unusual as you imagine," Thorn said. "I learned the ordinary skills any boy should know. How to fish and snare game and how to read the stars."

"Ah," Raven said. "Then we shall not get lost, wherever we wander."

"Turnabout is fair play," Thorn said, anxious to change the subject lest he reveal too much.

"I am a child of the air," Raven declared, "half mortal, half spirit, born beneath a giant mushroom in the forest of the fairy folk. I was reared in a hollow tree by an old witchy-woman who taught me all I know."

"A happy accident to meet you on this road," Thorn said, delighted by Raven's fanciful tale.

"Nothing happens by accident." Raven eyed Thorn's bulging pack. "I could do with a bite to eat. I have a pot for cooking, but alas, nothing to put in it! Would there be any meat in there, or only things for making snares and catching fish?"

Thorn laughed. "I will share this evening's meal, and we will set a snare for the morrow."

When the sun went down, they stopped in a clearing beside the road and Thorn opened his pack, taking out more of Morwid's berries and the dried venison. The travelers ate in companionable silence, listening to the night sounds. When they had eaten their fill, Thorn walked farther into the forest and chose a place to set his snare. He baited it and covered it with loose brush, and returned to find Raven bent over his pack, studying the arrow, bowl, and shell. Thorn's fingers tightened on the handle of his dirk.

"Get away from there!" he yelled. "What a fool I am! I should have known you for a thief."

Raven carefully replaced the shell he had been holding. "I cannot blame you for thinking poorly of me, but I am *not* a thief." He gestured toward Thorn's pack. "Earth, air, and water. And there in your hand the dirk, born of fire. It is as I believed when first I set my eyes upon you. You are no ordinary traveler, Thorn, but someone on a quest. And I know what it is you seek."

Blood pounded in Thorn's ears. Gone from Morwid for only a day and night, and already he had been found out! He was angrier at his own stupidity than he was at

Raven for pilfering his things and deducing the truth.

Raven crossed the clearing. "Forgive me for deceiving you, but I could not reveal the whole truth until I was sure of your identity. Now I am certain. You are the one." He indicated a spot behind Thorn's ear. "You have a birthmark, just there. In the shape of a thorn."

Thorn shivered. He supposed Raven could have spied his birthmark while they were traveling, though Thorn's long hair covered it completely. Could this strange boy truly be an enchanted child of the fairy folk?

Raven said, "You are wondering whether the story of my birth is true. Part of it is true, part of it is legend, but you must never doubt this: I have come to aid you in your quest."

"But how did you know? The Book of Ancients—" Thorn blurted before remembering that the very existence of the book was a secret.

"Says nothing about your birthmark," Raven finished. "Among my people there are many ways of knowing things." Placing a hand on Thorn's shoulder, Raven continued, "I did not need magic to discern who you are. The contents of your pack gave it away. But don't worry. Your secret is safe with me. Go ahead. Set me some test to prove my loyalty. I will do anything you say." Then, spying Thorn's fierce expression, Raven hastily amended, "Within reason, of course. I should not like to gouge out my eye or chop off my foot, but anything short of mayhem I will do."

Thorn sheathed his dirk, his head spinning. He could think of no task for this odd boy who seemed to possess strange powers. "How do you know all this?"

"That is of no consequence," Raven said. "The important thing is to find the amulet, is it not?"

"Aye." Though Raven seemed sincere, Thorn couldn't help remembering Drucilla's vision. *Two as one.* Would Raven join the quest for the amulet, only to claim it for himself? If Raven truly were enchanted, he might well take the amulet and disappear into thin air.

"Come and sleep now," Raven said, patting the ground beside him, "for a long journey awaits us on the morrow." His expression seemed so guileless, his concern for Thorn so genuine, that Thorn set aside his suspicions, deciding to wait until they reached the summer country to make up his mind about Raven.

Thorn slept so soundly that it seemed only minutes had passed before the sun came glimmering through the trees, rousing him and his companion from sleep. Before he could greet Raven, on the road there appeared another traveler, a boy in scarlet breeches and cloak, with a lute slung carelessly over his shoulder.

"A music maker!" Raven exclaimed with a wide grin. "Oh, this journey promises to be a pleasant one indeed."

He scrambled to his feet and made a sweeping bow. "Good day!" he called before Thorn could collect himself. "Come! Share some bread, and then we shall have a song or two to start this day's journey."

The boy removed his hat and returned Raven's bow. "Every day should begin with bread and song," he said. "Roger Tuckett's the name. From Arondale by way of Wyr."

Thorn nodded to the newcomer, but he was filled with uneasiness. Surely it was best not to let too many know of his quest. But there was Raven bidding the traveler to sit down, chattering away as if the musician were his own long-lost brother. Thorn sighed. There was nothing to be done about it now except share their food and wish the traveler a pleasant journey. But he intended to warn Raven about such encounters in the future.

"This is my friend Thorn," Raven said to the scarlet-clad boy. "I am called Raven."

Roger Tuckett set aside his lute and clasped their hands in turn. "I am pleased beyond words to find you here, for I do not fancy traveling one step farther upon this road."

"A dangerous way is it?" Raven asked, offering the boy a chunk of bread.

Roger gobbled the bread and reached for more. "You have not heard? Folks call this the Road of

Misfortune, for unpleasant things have happened to many a traveler hereabouts."

"Mayhap I should cast a spell to keep us safe," Raven said. He smiled to show he was joking, but Thorn was filled with a sense that Raven could do precisely that, if he so decided. His head swam with the very strangeness of the situation. Why had Morwid not warned him of the danger awaiting him on this road?

Roger wiped his hands on his cloak and studied Thorn. "'Golden hair and golden eye,'" he murmured. "It must be true. You are indeed the one. The sun seeker."

"The sun seeker?" Thorn frowned, feeling more confused than ever. It was as if he were in the middle of a fevered dream where everything had gone topsy-turvy.

Roger took up his lute and played a plaintive tune. "You are on a quest for a lost treasure, though you are not certain exactly what it looks like. Is that not so?"

Raven jumped up. "Have some more bread!"

A smile played on Roger's lips. "Your attempt to distract me is noble, my friend, but it will not work, for the story of the sun seeker is well known in Wyr."

Wyr. Thorn remembered Morwid's story of the battle that the king of Wyr fought against Kelhadden, in which the amulet was lost. Now, forgetting his caution, he said, "What can you tell me about the treasure? Can you describe it?"

"Not that we have anything more than a passing

interest in it," Raven said hastily, shooting Thorn a warning look. "Such a mystery is always the object of curiosity, is it not?"

Another tune rose from the lute while Roger thought. Then he said, "Deep inside the castle at Wyr there lies hidden a seeing stone. I have never looked upon it myself, but it is said the stone foretells a golden-haired one who must find the sun."

"But that is nonsense!" Thorn said, gesturing toward the sky. "For there lies the sun in plain sight. You make no sense at all!"

Roger shrugged. "I know what I know." Taking up his lute, he sang:

> *"Half then whole.*
> *Half then whole.*
> *Thief of light that goes by night*
> *shall with its twin*
> *restore the right."*

Abruptly Roger rose and bowed. "I thank you for the breakfast and wish you safe journey. As for me, I shall betake myself another way, for my purpose upon this road is done."

"Wait!" Thorn cried. "What purpose? What have you done except confuse my mind and fill my heart with worry?"

"What have I done? Why, given you a clue to your future," Roger said. "Though you may not think so just now, find the missing half and I promise you will know it. And now, good day."

With that, he turned and disappeared around the bend in the road.

Thorn stared at Raven, his mind teeming with all he had just heard. "The missing half?" he said to Raven. "A sun seeker? I am sorely troubled. I should not have asked so many questions."

"This morn is off to a worrisome start," Raven agreed. "But what's done is done. Let us see whether your snare has yielded anything good to eat. We will need more than a crust of bread to fill our bellies, and problems are more manageable after a goodly meal."

It was true that his stomach was complaining quite loudly, so Thorn walked into the brush to check his snare. He removed the hare he'd caught, then sat down on a boulder to think. He had trusted Morwid to give him everything necessary for his quest, but now it seemed the most important thing—knowledge—was missing, and he didn't know where to find it.

"Thorn!" Raven's voice echoed through the trees. "Gypsies! Come quick!"

Thorn ran to the clearing and peered down the road. A colorful band of dark-skinned travelers was approaching in a horse-drawn wagon laden with pots and pans, with lutes and tambourines that twanged and rattled with every turn of the wheels. Holding the reins was a man in a red turban. Beside him sat a young girl in red skirts and an armful of bracelets. Six pairs of dark eyes peered from inside the wagon as it neared the clearing. The turbaned man called out, "Halloooo!"

Raven raised a hand in greeting. Beside him stood Thorn, still holding the hare.

"Fresh game!" the man said to Thorn, halting the wagon. "I don't suppose you would consider sharing with us?" He jumped off the wagon and rubbed his hands together as if anticipating a bountiful feast.

"It won't feed so many," Thorn said warily as the six children, all chattering at once, spilled from the wagon like ants from an anthill.

"True enough," the man said, "but it would flavor the pot of onion soup my daughter made this morn. It has been too long since we tasted meat."

The children eyed the hare longingly. With their thin faces and hollow expressions, they reminded Thorn of the starving, ragtag band of forest people he had vowed to save. The appearance of yet more strangers on the Road of Misfortune made him uneasy, and his own belly was empty too, but he couldn't ignore the need staring him right in the face. He was a prince now and obliged to help others less fortunate.

The man went on, "We have no coins for payment,

but we would please you with a song and a magic trick or two. Or mayhap you would have your fortune told. My daughter is the best in all the land at seeing into the future."

The girl with the armload of bracelets blushed and smiled shyly. "Oh, Papa."

"She is too modest," her father said. "Once, the duke of Fernym summoned us all the way from our village just to hear her predictions."

Thorn picked up his skinning knife. "We will share with you, but then we must be away, for we have important business in the summer country."

"By fortunate coincidence, we are headed in the same direction!" the man said. "Our wagon is a bit crowded, but we would be happy to have you ride along."

Eager to be rid of the strangers, Thorn said, "There is no need for—"

Before he could finish, Raven shook the man's hand and said, "We accept! My shoe leather is worn thin as paper, and I am tired of sleeping on the ground. The sooner we reach a village, the better."

"Half a day's journey will bring us to Allswell," the man said. "'Tis so small a village it hardly deserves the name, but there is a tavern and a place to rest your bones."

And so it was that by late morning the children were

full of rabbit stew and the last of the bread, and Thorn and Raven were riding atop the jostling wagon as it neared the village.

"I can see this man spoke rightly," Raven muttered to Thorn. "There is aught here but a few huts. And the tavern."

"I hope they have a pudding there," Thorn said. "I cannot remember the last time I had one."

The wagon stopped just short of the village, and the gypsy man called over his shoulder, "The likes of us are not welcome in town. You'd best go on alone."

As Thorn gathered his belongings, the girl with the bracelets suddenly grasped his palm and peered into it. She stared, then blanched and dropped Thorn's hand as quickly as she had seized it.

"Bad news, daughter?" the man asked.

The girl swallowed. "I see . . . death. And soon."

Raven grabbed Thorn's arm and they jumped off the wagon. Before they could say their good-byes, the man flicked the reins and the wagon careered around the curve.

Thorn stared after them, unsettled by the girl's dire prediction.

"Do not give her words another thought," Raven said, as if reading Thorn's mind. "They mean nothing. Anyone can predict death, or a long journey or a happy surprise, and be right sooner or later."

Thorn's pent-up breath whooshed out of his lungs and at last he grinned. "Of course you are right. 'Tis a confounding day, what with that strange Roger Tuckett and then the gypsies."

"We need a pudding and a soft bed," Raven said. "And some entertainment to ease our cares. We will feel better on the morrow."

With that, they entered Allswell, but Thorn saw at once that the rest they sought was not to be. The tavern was closed. Along the cobbled street, doors stood open; the shops and sellers' stalls were unattended. The villagers were crowded onto the green to witness a flogging. The hapless thief, his pilfered goods still piled at his feet, was stripped to the waist and tied by hands and feet over a large barrel. A pale young woman, swollen with child, stood near the edge of the crowd weeping, her hands stretched toward the young thief.

A burly man in a leather coat and breeches strode through the crowd, his whip at the ready. Bile rose in Thorn's throat. Witnessing yet more cruelty, albeit for thieving, was more than he could bear.

"Come away," he said to Raven, and they made their way around the edge of the noisy throng. A roar went up from the villagers as the flogging began. Thorn blocked it from his mind and led Raven up a hillside till they reached a meadow. There he dropped his pack and sat down on the grass. The events of the day had left him tired, hungry, and full of doubt. Why had Roger Tuckett called him the sun seeker? It made no more sense than the riddle about the thief of light. And the terrified look in the gypsy girl's eyes as she read his palm was no pretense. She believed in the veracity of her prediction, even if he did not.

Raven took out his flute and blew a few sweet notes. "The tavern will be open again once the flogging is done," he said. "Then we will have a hot meal and a long rest before we continue our journey. Now, quiet your mind. All will be fine anon." He waved one arm toward the village. "After all, are we not in a town called Allswell?"

CHAPTER FIVE

"How much farther to the summer country?" Thorn asked one afternoon as he and Raven crossed a shallow streamed and continued down the road. Since leaving Allswell, they had walked for days, meeting only an occasional horseman or a farmer driving his oxcart. Already the autumn rains had given way to frost; soon would come snow and bitter cold.

Raven glanced at the mottled sky, then sniffed the air, turned in a circle, and clapped his hands three times. "Methinks this road will end by nightfall, and soon we will reach the summer country."

Thorn had long since given up trying to understand how Raven divined such things. "I hope so," he said, quickening his pace, "for I wish to be done with this Road of Misfortune before bad luck catches up with us."

Though Raven had comported himself like a true and loyal friend, Thorn couldn't stop thinking about Drucilla's admonitions, Roger Tuckett's puzzling riddle, and the gypsy girl's terrible prediction.

"'Tis never wise to press one's luck too far," Raven agreed. He took out his flute. "Too bad you forgot your own flute, Thorn. I should have liked hearing you play."

"You play much more sweetly than I," Thorn said truthfully. "Make a merry song, if you will, to speed this day along."

And so Raven played one tune and then another until, toward evening, a scattering of rooftops appeared on the horizon. As the first part of his journey was ending, Thorn's uneasiness returned. Soon he must enter a strange world with only his dreams for guidance. But he walked steadily onward, till at last they entered a village teeming with farmers, dairymaids, ironmongers, and merchants, all hawking their wares.

As they passed a ribbon seller's stall, a girl in a hooded cloak caught Thorn's eye and smiled. He halted his steps and stared. Looking at her was like gazing into a still pond. Her oval face, high forehead, and tawny eyes perfectly mirrored his own. *The missing half.*

"Raven!" he cried. "That girl looks just like me!"

Raven looked in the direction Thorn pointed, but when Thorn looked again, the girl had vanished, as quickly as a wisp of wood smoke. "Perhaps it was merely a trick of the light," Raven said. "Let's go. I hear music."

Near the inn a troupe of musicians was performing in the courtyard. As the boys walked toward the sound, Thorn looked over his shoulder for another glimpse of the girl, but she was lost in the crowd. When they reached the courtyard, Raven took out his flute and joined in the song making. Before Thorn knew quite what was happening, a pink-faced milkmaid grabbed his arm and twirled him around and around in a lively dance that left him breathless and dizzy. His pack and quiver jounced up and down as he and the milkmaid turned this way and that. The crowd clapped their hands and the milkmaid laughed out loud, but Thorn was thinking only of the golden-eyed girl. He felt drawn to her as if by a magic spell. He searched for her in the crowd of merrymakers as he and the milkmaid dipped and whirled.

Then the door to the inn flew open and a red-faced man, puffed up like a turkey-cock, rushed out. "Stop! Stop this infernal racket!"

He seized Thorn's tunic and brought him up short. The musicians stopped playing midnote. The milkmaid turned and ran.

"Have you no brains?" the man shouted at Thorn. "My guests are tired and would rest before they sup, if not for this abominable noise."

The hot, sour smell rising from the man's clothes made Thorn's nose burn, but he said politely, "Begging your pardon, Sir. We meant no harm."

Raven stepped between them and said to the innkeeper, "'Tis I and the other music makers who caused the disturbance, and we do beg your forgiveness." With a courtly bow he said, "I am called Raven."

"Appropriate for one who offends our ears with such harsh sounds." The man made a shooing motion. "Go on! Away with the lot of you." He stomped inside and slammed the door.

"Never mind him," said a voice at Thorn's elbow. He turned to find the girl from the ribbon seller's stall smiling at him.

Raven doffed his hat and bowed to her. "You are not a trick of the light after all."

Before Thorn could speak, the girl said, "Never mind the innkeeper. Old March is blustery as his name, but not so fierce as he sounds, as I learned when I arrived yestereve. The inn was full, but he let me sleep on the floor and would not take even the smallest coin in payment."

She removed her cloak, and Thorn saw that her hair, worn in a thick braid down her back, was the exact color of his own. She wore leather boots, a man's tunic and breeches, and a dirk sheathed at her waist. "Come," she said to Thorn. "We must find a place to talk, for I can see you are fairly bursting with questions."

"That church over there will be just the place," Raven said, nodding toward a meadow.

The three left the courtyard and hurried along the street, then crossed the meadow to the church that stood alone beneath a grove of oaks. The moment they were inside, Thorn tossed his pack onto the floor and seized the girl's arm. "Who are you?"

"I am called Lira." She smiled serenely, then planted a kiss on Thorn's cheek. "I have long waited for this day, my brother."

"Brother?" Thorn released her and stared, bewildered, first at her, then at Raven. His chest filled with relief, joy, and an unspeakable sweetness. Had the old yearning at last found its answer? A thirst to know everything about her, about himself, welled up inside him. He swallowed the lump forming in his throat.

Lira unbound her hair, and it settled in a shimmering golden sheet across her shoulders. "Surely you see the resemblance now," she said. "In truth we are more than mere siblings, Thorn, for we were born the same day and hour, though our mother says I came first into the world, so that makes me the elder twin."

"But . . . Morwid gave me my name. How do you know it?" He turned to Raven. "If this is some trick you have concocted to amuse me, it has failed miserably, for I do not like being fooled."

"It is no trick," Lira said quietly. "I have seen you before, and yet I have not."

"You speak in riddles!" Thorn cried.

"Thorn." Raven put his hand on his friend's shoulder. "Your twin possesses the gift of sight."

Lira nodded. "Sometimes I can see things that are happening far away as clearly as if they were unfolding right before my eyes. 'Tis quite unsettling."

Thorn rounded on Raven. "You knew this all along, yet you said nothing? Why am I the last to know everything? Why did you not tell me of my other half?"

"The time was not yet right," Raven said in a manner that reminded Thorn of Drucilla.

"And you are a seer!" Thorn said to Lira. He went on staring at this marvelous creature. Everything in the world seemed new and strange now that he had found her. "Pray tell, what things do you see?"

Lira dropped her cloak onto a bench and sat facing Thorn, her hands folded primly on her lap. "Most often it is a vision of someone known to me, and most often the person is in some kind of danger." Tears welled in her eyes. "That is the worst of it, Thorn, to know someone is in peril and yet be unable to help. More than once I have wished you were the one our mother had trained to this gift."

Unexpectedly Thorn's own eyes filled. He could not understand why their mother had not kept them both.

As if reading his jumbled thoughts, Lira said, "You must not think badly of her. Often she spoke of how bitterly she wept for you when the maid came to take you away. But you see, our father—"

"Ranulf?" Thorn whispered, wanting to know and yet dreading the answer.

"Aye. He would have killed you on sight, since you are a twin, which some think portends evil in both mother and child."

Remembering his encounter with Ranulf the night Morwid was wounded, Thorn nodded. "He seems to have treated you well enough. Though in those clothes I would never have known you for a princess."

"I left the abbey suddenly. It was either this or a nun's habit. Granted, this costume does not look like much, but 'tis more comfortable than long robes and a wimple."

"The abbey?" Thorn let out a long sigh. "I am more confused than ever."

Raven spread his cloak upon the floor and plopped down, cross-legged, in front of the twins. "Methinks we should make ourselves comfortable, for this promises to be a long tale indeed." To Lira he said, "Do begin at the beginning, Princess."

"The beginning. When Ranulf deposed King Warn, he married our mother, Isotta. She was King Warn's daughter and the treasure of her father's heart."

"She promised to marry the Northman to spare her father a life in the dungeon," Thorn supplied.

"Then, you know that part of the story."

Raven said, "Go on, Lira. Tell us all that has happened since."

"Well," Lira continued, warming quickly to her story, "the night we were born, a red fire appeared in the sky. Watching the heavens from her bedchamber window, our mother saw, and right away she knew it for a sign. Someday her son would find the king's lost amulet and save Kelhadden. She dared not let our father know, so when I was born first, the nurse wrapped me in swaddling and took me to show to him. While Ranulf was occupied, our mother summoned one of her maids with instructions to spirit you from the castle and leave you near the cave of King Warn's old counselor, Morwid, who Mother thought was both kind and wise."

"Aye." A wave of homesickness washed over Thorn. "He is a hard one to understand, but he has been both mother and father to me. And now he is wounded by Ranulf's own hand."

Lira nodded, unsurprised. "Not more than a fortnight ago I saw you in a vision with our father upon a darkened path, and there were two others with him. Then I felt a hard stinging on my cheek, cold and sharp as ice, and I knew you were hurt."

"He meant to kill Morwid," Thorn said, amazed at his twin's gift. "And he boxed my ears till I nearly saw stars. But how did you—"

Lira touched her cheek. "I cannot explain it. Once or twice I have felt such a strong oneness between us that when you wept, I tasted salt. But many times I have tried to summon you with no luck at all."

Thorn tried to take it all in, but he was still thinking about the mother he had never known. "Was our mother visiting the abbey with you? Where is she now?"

A sudden commotion outside the church forestalled Lira's reply.

"Stop, thief!" someone shouted. Thorn, Raven, and Lira rushed to the window. March, the innkeeper, ran across the meadow, chasing a long-haired dwarf whose rough wool cape billowed behind him like a sail. Though the boy moved with an awkward, crablike gait, he was much too fast for March. The innkeeper gave up the chase in the middle of the meadow, his fist raised against the sky. "Stay away from my inn, if you know what is good for you!" he yelled.

The odd-looking boy passed beneath the grove of trees and threw open the church door. Spying Thorn and Lira, he stopped short and blinked his eyes. "What ho! Do my eyes fail me? I would swear there are two of you, but mayhap 'tis only the ale I had for breakfast."

Thorn stepped forward and regarded the newcomer through narrowed eyes. "Though all are welcome in church, I hope you are not truly a thief."

Reaching into his pocket, the boy said, "All I took was an apple for my supper, and a wormy one at that, but the way old March carried on, one would think I had stolen the crown jewels and the royal treasury besides." He polished the apple on his sleeve and took a bite. "So," he said, his gooseberry eyes flitting from Thorn to Lira and then to Raven, "it's obvious these two are twins, and who might you be?"

"I am called Raven. This is Thorn and his sister, Lira. We are on our way to the summer country."

"Truly?" The boy swallowed his bite of apple and sucked his teeth. "I am Baldric. As it happens, I am on my way there myself. Suppose we pass the night in this church and set out together on the morrow, for there be safety in numbers."

Thorn, his usual caution muted by curiosity, was about to agree, but Lira spoke first. "Why should you need our protection?"

"I thought you might need mine, girl, but I see now you possess both a dirk and a bold spirit. Never mind. Forget I ever mentioned it."

"Mayhap my sister spoke hastily," Thorn said. "If it

be agreeable to you, we should be glad of your company."

Baldric grinned. "Splendid! Now, what's for supper? I am hungry as a bear in springtime."

While Raven and Lira spread a blanket on the floor next to Raven's cloak, Thorn, eager for his twin to continue her story, gave Baldric a strip of dried meat and some berries from his pack. The dwarf smacked his lips and popped the berries into his mouth.

Raven and Lira ate their meal with obvious enjoyment, but Thorn was too excited by the day's events to swallow more than a few bites. Baldric gobbled his food as if he were starving, then curled up in a corner and covered himself with his cloak. Raven donned his own cloak and went out to check the weather.

Lira clutched her twin's arm and propelled him to the back of the church. "Why on earth did you agree to travel with him, Thorn?" she demanded in a fierce whisper. "I smell trouble."

"He *is* an odd one, but he seems harmless. And since we don't know our way through the summer country, he may be of some use. Unless, of course, you can *see* our way to that far place."

Anger darkened Lira's eyes. "I came here because I thought you needed my help, but it seems I was mistaken. On the morrow I shall return to the abbey and leave you to your own devices."

"Return to the abbey? You do not live with our parents in the castle?"

"Not since the day Father caught Mother and me practicing my art." Her irritation with her brother seemingly forgotten, Lira went on. "We were in my bedchamber, where I had cast a circle of flame for the first time. Truly, I could not tell which shone brighter, the candles or Mother's face. She was very proud of me. A friend of hers, a seer called Drucilla, had sent me a sphere of malachite, meant to help focus the mind—"

"Morwid's friend!" Thorn exclaimed, delighted to have found something in common with his twin. "I met her myself on the night Ranulf attacked us on the trail."

"Is she well?" Lira asked. "I fear for the lives of everyone in Kelhadden these days."

"She is well," Thorn said, "though quite frail. She says her powers are fading."

"That will be a loss for everyone who depends on her," Lira said. "If you have met Drucilla, then you know what a brokenhearted soul she is. Mother told me Drucilla's only grandchild was given up for safekeeping when the Northmen came. When I think of all the misery our father has caused, I can scarcely bear to know it is his blood running in my veins."

In his corner of the church Baldric shifted, mumbled, and began snoring. Raven returned, chafing his arms. "'Tis a brisk wind that blows tonight," he said.

"Methinks we shall have snow before this month is through." He handed Thorn a cup of water. "For your dream potion."

"My thanks, Raven, but I won't need the potion just yet. Drucilla said to drink it once I reach the summer country. I must get there soon if I am to save the forest people."

"Indeed you must," Lira said. "Our own mother lives among them now."

Thorn stared at his twin. "I saw her!" he said, his voice low and full of wonder. "It was on the night of Ranulf's attack. Morwid took me to the forest to see Drucilla. Then, to convince me of my destiny, he showed me the forest people and sent me to a hollow stump to leave meat for them. A woman came out of the shadows, silent as a ghost, and touched my arm. It *was* our mother. I am certain of it."

"Did she speak to you?" Raven asked. "Did she call your name?"

"I *felt* her greeting, though I did not recognize her then."

Lira said, "How did she seem, Thorn? Does she fare well?"

"You would know that better than I."

"I wish it were so, but it has been more than five years since our last meeting, and though I have tried to summon a vision of her, I cannot."

"Go on," Thorn urged. "How did you come to leave the castle?"

"Well, as I said, Ranulf came into my bedchamber and saw my circle of flame. He thought we meant to cast upon him an evil spell. He shouted to Mother that he would see us both in chains before sunrise and then left my room without another word. I suppose he thought we were too frightened of him to flee, but Mother bundled me into my cloak, and we left the castle within the hour and went to Saint Anne's. The abbess, a cousin to my old nurse, kindly took us in."

"'Tis a wonder you were safe, even there," Thorn said.

"Not even Ranulf is base enough to attack a church. Mother left me there and went to help the forest people, though I hear from the occasional visitor that there is little anyone can do for them."

Raven stifled a yawn. "The hour grows late. I need sleep. You must rest as well, my prince."

"I am too excited for sleep," Thorn said.

"I'm not sleepy either." Lira squeezed her twin's arm. "Let us walk awhile."

She picked up her cloak. The twins left the church and crossed the meadow to a crumbling wall that lay close to the ground. Lira perched there and drew her cloak about her shoulders. Above them the moon hung like a bright opal in the inky sky, its light washing over the stone buildings.

"Tell me everything!" Thorn hoisted himself onto the wall beside her. "All my life I felt as if something important was missing, and now I have found it."

"What would you like to know?"

"Tell me about Kelhadden," Thorn urged. "I have wondered what it is like to live in a castle."

"It was not so pleasant as you might imagine," Lira began. "Mostly I tried to avoid Father's vile temper and to spare myself his tedious war tales." She brushed a strand of hair from her eyes. "I do miss my bedchamber, though. At night it was lit with a dozen shining candles. There was a carpet to warm my feet, and a feather bed with a blue coverlet. At the abbey there is aught but a blanket on the floor and a bucket of cold water for washing."

"At least you are free of Ranulf there," Thorn said.

"When you find the amulet, we all shall be free of him."

Then Thorn again felt the weight of his great burden. "Despite all Morwid taught me, I fear I am not prepared for the task," he confided. "The harder I look for answers, the more questions I find. Suppose I fail. What then?"

"Mother says a thousand hardships must not cause a single doubt. You can't give up your quest, no matter how difficult it seems." Lira paused. "Now it is your turn. Tell me about your journey."

As the night wind swept the meadow and the moon made its way across the heavens, Thorn described the Road of Misfortune and his meetings with the band of gypsies and with Roger Tuckett. Thorn recited the bard's strange song about the thief of light.

"He claimed to have given me the key to my future," Thorn said, "but it makes no sense at all."

"Once, a band of minstrels came to the castle and played nonsense tunes until Father heard and threw them out," Lira said. "Perhaps Roger Tuckett meant the song merely as entertainment."

"I don't think so," Thorn said, his expression troubled. "I hope Drucilla's potion will guide me when the time comes."

"I am certain it will." Lira shivered and yawned. "The moon is setting and still I am too happy for sleep. I can hardly wait till the Northmen are banished and we can go home together."

She clasped her brother's hands and saw by his shining eyes that he felt exactly the same. The twins sat for a moment longer, watching the night sky. The breeze lifted their hair, and the golden strands mingled in the darkness.

❧ CHAPTER SIX ❧

ARMS AKIMBO, LIRA GLARED AT HER TWIN. "DID I NOT tell you that dwarf was trouble? Morwid may have trained you in the arts of war, my brother, but you are woefully ignorant of human nature. By the saints, I do not know what we will do now."

They had wakened early to find the strange boy gone, pack and all, and with him Thorn's dream potion.

Lira's words stung. Of course Thorn could see now how foolish he had been, but it was too late to undo the damage. Worse, the warm feeling that had passed between him and his twin the night before had vanished along with the dwarf. "Go back to the abbey, then," he said coldly. "I will find the amulet somehow."

"You would have trouble finding your own back-side!"

Raven stepped between the twins. "May the saints protect me from stinging nettles and quarrelsome princesses!" He frowned at Thorn. "It will not do to battle among ourselves. We must think only of our kingdom and how to get it back from the Northmen." He turned to Lira. "Can you make another dream potion to guide us?"

"I helped Mother make potions from time to time. I suppose I could try. If you truly want my help."

Eager to regain his twin's good graces, Thorn said, "I have comfrey and balsam."

"A good beginning," Lira said. "If only we could find a garden . . ."

"Methinks I know just the place," Raven said. "On the way into the village yestereve I spied a fine house set amid a meadow. You remember it, Thorn."

"I remember it, and also the iron gate and sturdy wall that guards it round about."

"Merely a slight inconvenience," Raven said with a wave of his hand. "We can be over it and back in a trice."

"I suppose, but what if there is no garden?"

Raven laughed. "You might as well ask, What if there is no spring? Tell me true, have you ever seen a house that fine without a garden?"

"No, but then, I lived all my life in a cave," Thorn said.

Lira paused in her gathering up of their packs and cloaks. "Raven is right. That house must have some kind of garden."

"Come on, then, before the town awakes." Thorn donned his cloak and shouldered his pack and quiver.

They left the church, crossed the meadow, and turned onto the street. At March's inn a single candle glowed in the darkened window. A horse bearing a cloaked rider raced past. Somewhere far off a dog barked. They hurried down the road. Twisted shadows lay across their path as they crossed the meadow and crept along the hedge till they reached the house, and the wall.

Thorn handed Lira his pack for safekeeping, then inquired, his voice low, "Can you whistle?"

Lira merely rolled her eyes.

He grinned. "Keep a sharp eye out, then, and whistle us a warning should anyone approach."

Raven quickly shed his cloak. He spat on his hands and whispered to Lira, "What shall we fetch for you, milady, for making the dream potion?"

"I am well able to climb this wall and get them for myself, but since you seem eager to do my bidding, I need sage for wisdom and more balsam for calming the mind. Some bloodrose and white fern, unless the frost has withered it."

Thorn knelt in the shadow of the wall. Raven climbed onto his shoulders and sprang lightly onto the top, then grasped Thorn's hands and pulled him up.

"Well?" Lira whispered. "Can you see a garden?"

"Miles of gardens," Thorn reported. "And ponds full of sleeping ducks and swans."

Just then an ominous growl came from the shadows. "Dogs, too," murmured Raven. "Watch how you go, Thorn."

Silently the boys edged along the wall till they reached the garden, then dropped to the ground. On his knees in the dirt, Thorn moved among the plants, pulling up handfuls of balsam and sage. He looked about with some uncertainty for the bloodrose. Morwid had never spoken of that plant and its uses.

"Methinks this must be it." Raven held up a red flower with drooping petals. "But I do not see anything that looks like white—"

"Grrrrrrrrrrr-arf!" A streak of black tore across the garden and latched on to Thorn's breeches. Thorn stifled a yell as he went down, rolling over and over with the snarling dog.

"Off, you miserable cur!" he muttered fiercely, but the dog held on.

From the other side of the fence Lira gave a piercing whistle.

Raven grabbed the dog's neck and met its eyes.

"*Abzecram,*" he said, keeping his voice low. "*Lorwit.*"

In an instant the dog released Thorn, whimpered, and lay down at Raven's feet.

Thorn gathered his herbs, dusted himself off, and stared at Raven. "How did you do that?"

Then came another frantic whistle from Lira.

"Quick!" Raven cried. "Over the wall!"

The boys scrambled up and jumped a thorny hedge just as the iron gate swung wide with an ear-piercing creak. A burly man, still in his nightclothes, ran out brandishing a sputtering torch in one hand and a dirk in the other. Three more growling dogs trailed behind him. "Halt, you wretched thieves," he yelled, "before I set the hounds on you!"

"Run!" Lira yelled. The three snatched up their packs and raced pell-mell across the road and deep into the wood, the dogs baying and nipping at their heels. Farther and farther they ran, until at last the dogs gave up the chase.

Raven leaned against a tree and wiped his brow. "By the saints! There was no time to tame those three curs. I thought they had us."

"That was close," Thorn agreed as the three stood panting, waiting to recover their breath. A searing pain had begun in his leg, just above the top of his boot. He winced as a trickle of blood ran down his calf.

"You're hurt!" Lira cried.

"'Tis but a scratch," Thorn said bravely.

"Even so, it's foolhardy to ignore it," Lira declared. "Suppose you fall ill. Then where will we be?"

She looked so fierce Thorn couldn't help smiling. "Begging your pardon, my princess," he said, making an exaggerated bow. "I am properly chastised."

Lira laughed. She was finding it impossible to stay angry with Thorn for very long. From a hawthorn bush she extracted a cobweb and pressed it into Thorn's wound. As she bent to her task, a necklace worn beneath her tunic swung free. Made of a crescent-shaped bit of crystal, it caught and reflected the rising sun, splintering the light.

Seeing Thorn's interest in it, she held it out for his inspection. "'Tis very old, our mother says. It was her parting gift to me the night she left me at the abbey. No more than a trifle, the abbess says, but precious to me all the same."

"It reminds me of the moon," Thorn said.

"I suppose."

Before he could think on it further, Lira straightened and tucked the necklace inside her tunic. "Your wound is bound, my brother. Now, pray tell, what did you find in the garden?"

Handing her the herbs and the red flower, he said, "I hope this is the bloodrose, for I have never before seen one."

"A good guess. Now I can make a new potion."

Raven righted his feathered hat and said, "Can it possibly wait until we've eaten? I cannot think properly when my belly is growling. I am empty all the way to my toes."

Lira packed away her herbs for safekeeping, and they set off through the woods. By the time they regained the road and returned to the village, the streets were once again alive with people and geese, oxcarts and horses. The door to March's inn stood open, and the smells of frying bacon and porridge wafted out.

Thorn said to Lira, "I thought Morwid had given me everything I needed for this task, but I have no money. Have you any coins, or must we work for our breakfast?"

From the folds of her tunic Lira produced a fat leather pouch. "Borrowed from the collection box at Saint Anne's. I didn't think the abbess would mind, so long as we repay her when our journey is done."

"Fair enough," Raven said. "Dare we show ourselves at the innkeeper's table, or shall we take our chances with yestermorn's bread and a bit of cheese from some cart?"

"March will be glad enough to serve us once he sees Lira's coins," Thorn said. "Mayhap at the inn we can learn of Baldric's whereabouts. I want to get my potion back, else that little thief will find the amulet first."

So saying, he motioned to Raven and Lira, and

they went in. All around the room the buzz of a dozen conversations suddenly died. Forks clattered onto plates. People stared. A woman screamed. A crone in a purple cloak jumped up and grabbed a handful of salt and frantically tossed it over her shoulder. "Evil!" she shouted, pointing one crooked, bony finger at the twins. "Be gone! Out! Out!"

Then the innkeeper rushed into the room, a towel slung over his shoulder. "By all that is holy, Eleanor!" he cried. "What is the matter with you?"

"Twins!" the crone yelled. "Pure evil! You'd better get them out of here, March, before something horrible happens."

The one called Eleanor gathered up her bundle and hurried away. Two men at a corner table shoved their plates aside and followed her. Another woman pushed past the twins on her way out the door.

March studied Thorn's face. "It's you!" he said. "The one who disturbed the peace in the courtyard yesterday."

Before Thorn could reply, Raven pulled out his silver flute and blew a few sweet notes. "If you remember, Sir, it was I who made the noise. And I did most humbly apologize."

March grunted, then squinted at Lira. "I have seen you before as well."

Lira curtsied as sweetly as she could, given her odd

costume. "You let me sleep on your floor, Sir, and I am most grateful for your kindness."

"What do you want now?"

"Only something to eat, then we will be gone." Lira opened her pouch and took out a handful of coins. "We are willing to pay."

"Well . . ." March looked doubtful, but the shiny coins were too tempting to pass up. He scanned the room and finally said, "Take that table in the back, and don't call attention to yourselves. You're frightening my regular customers. I can't have that."

"No, Sir," Thorn said.

March turned on his heel and left the room, muttering to himself.

A serving girl with a thicket of red hair and eyes black as raisins hurried over with bowls of porridge, a crock of butter, and thick slices of bread. "I hope old Eleanor didn't frighten you," she said. "She fancies herself a seer and a spell maker, but hardly anyone pays attention." She studied the twins. "You are not truly of the devil, are you?"

Raven laughed and took off his cap. "Of course they're not."

Lira said to the girl, "I wish my hair were as pretty as yours."

The girl blushed and giggled.

Then Thorn said, "We seek an acquaintance of ours.

A rather odd-looking boy called Baldric. He is short and round. Walks like a crab."

"Eyes like gooseberries," Lira supplied.

"We saw him here yestereve, but now we have lost him," Raven said, buttering his bread.

"Ha!" said the serving girl. "That thief! He comes and goes like the weather. Most likely you will find him in the Valley of Sighs."

"And where might that be?" Thorn asked.

"Why, in the summer country, of course." She picked up three empty plates and a half-empty bowl of porridge from a nearby table. "If you find him, tell him I want my bracelet back. 'Tis all I have to remind me of my dear mother."

"The summer country," Thorn repeated. "Can you tell me how to find it?'

"Amice!" March bellowed from the other room. "What keeps you?"

"In a moment, Father!" The girl turned to Thorn. "Of course, I have never been there myself," she said hurriedly. "They say 'tis guarded by a most fearsome beast, but if you truly wish to find it . . ."

"We do," Lira said between spoonfuls of porridge.

"Very well. Behind the tanner's stall at the end of this road is a path leading through a wood. Follow it till you come to a tunnel covered with ivy. Beyond the tunnel you will find a river."

"Amice!"

"Coming! When you have crossed the river, you will be in the summer country," said the girl in a rush. "Of course, Baldric may be anywhere. Now, I must go. Be careful of the beast!"

She bustled away, her arms full of dirty dishes.

"Well," Raven said, "since we must journey to the summer country anyway, methinks we should find this Valley of Sighs and take back what is yours, Thorn."

"Aye." Thorn finished his bread and licked his fingers clean. "I should like to cross that river before nightfall."

"Do you suppose the beast is real or merely some traveler's fanciful tale?" Raven wondered aloud.

"Real or imagined, the sooner we get to the summer country, the sooner the amulet will be ours." Thorn spoke with a bravery he did not feel. Suppose the beast *were* real? Would he be strong enough, clever enough, to defeat it?

"And the sooner we all can go home," Lira finished wistfully. "Oh, Thorn, I wish you had grown up with me in the castle. Of course, when our father was there, it was a fearsome place, for he is given to terrible fits of temper. But when he was away, Mother and I played games in the garden. She told wonderful stories of our grandfather, and we had sweet cakes and ale, even for breakfast."

"Sweet cakes and ale! While I had aught but salted fish and wild berries!" Thorn said.

"It has been a long while since I tasted sweet cakes myself," Lira said. "Ranulf hoards every good thing for himself. He does not care one whit for the suffering of others. Even at the abbey we had only gruel and milk, and the occasional bit of mutton when there was a visitor brave enough to smuggle it inside."

Thorn nodded. "The forest people live on far less. If not for Morwid, they would be dead already."

"Tell me about him," Lira said.

Raven donned his yellow cap. "Save your tales for the journey, Thorn. The sun is up, and we must be away."

Lira left three coins on the table, and they went out into the crisp autumn morning. Raven sniffed the sky, turned in a circle, and clapped his hands three times. "Fair weather until the morrow," he said, and on that promise they shouldered their packs and set off for the summer country.

CHAPTER SEVEN

BEHIND THE TANNER'S STALL THEY FOUND THE PATH, precisely as the serving girl had described it. Soon they were in a deep wood, walking single file beneath a canopy of trees, Thorn in the lead, Raven bringing up the rear.

When they had walked some distance, Lira said to her brother, "Tell me about Morwid."

"Though I lived with him all my life, he still is a puzzlement," Thorn said. "Ofttimes his mind seemed so far away I could not tell what he was thinking. He is a keeper of secrets."

"And keeper of the Book of Ancients," Lira said. "Mother told me."

"He has vowed to return it to Kelhadden when Ranulf is defeated. From the day he found me lying in a basket outside his cave, he has prepared me for that task, but I learned of it only recently."

"That must have been a surprising bit of news."

Thorn stopped and pushed aside a leafy branch to clear the path for the others. "He is old as the sea and stubborn to a fault, but he is my only family."

Raven, who had been listening quietly, said, "That is not quite so. You have found your missing half, and soon you will have your mother as well."

"She weeps for you, Thorn," Lira said, her own eyes welling with tears. "Night and day she prays for your return."

Unaccustomed to such displays of feeling, Thorn said gruffly, "We must hurry. Enough time wasted on idle chatter."

"But still I know nothing of your life with Morwid!" Lira protested as they resumed walking.

"He loves a merry tale and a pleasing song," Thorn said, "though we had too little time for such things. In the evenings we held contests of strength and pretended to do battle with spears made of reeds, and he taught me the prophecies of the ancients."

The path dipped into a woodsy ravine, and soon they entered the tunnel the serving girl had described. Inside it was so dark they found their way only by holding on to one another as they inched along the path. Thorn wiped away the cobwebs that caught at his clothes, and batted at the furry creatures brushing his face as they crept through the tunnel.

Presently it narrowed till they could feel the walls against their shoulders as they passed. The air grew heavy and dank, and the ceiling seemed to press them down.

"How much farther?" Lira asked, though she knew none could answer that question.

"I should have lit a torch," Thorn said, himself eager for any glimmer of light. "I did not think this tunnel would be so long."

On they went, hour after hour, until they lost track of time. At last Thorn stopped suddenly. Lira and Raven fell against him. "Is it merely wishful thinking," Thorn said, "or do you see a point of light up ahead?"

"I see it!" Raven and Lira shouted together, and they quickened their steps, emerging at last from the blackness into a thick grove of trees. After so long in the darkness the dazzling sunlight hit them like a blow. Thorn shaded his eyes. Beyond the emerald forest lay a broad river, jeweled in sunlight.

"Oh!" Lira breathed. "How beautiful. It's like something in a fairy story or a wonderful dream."

"And no fearsome beast," Thorn said, hoping the others could not sense his profound relief.

Raven removed his cap and scratched his head. "On the other side of the river lies the summer country, but for the life of me, I cannot think how we can cross it."

"'Tis much too broad for swimming," Thorn decided.

"Well," Lira said brightly, "we have our two sharp dirks and a forest full of trees. We can build a raft."

"That will take far too long," Thorn said. "We must find Baldric right away and get my potion back. Not that I am ungrateful for your offer to make another, Lira, but what if it does not work?"

"I suppose you have a better idea?" Lira crossed her arms and stared at her twin.

Raven sighed. "Must the two of you disagree at every turn?"

"He will not listen to me," Lira complained, "though I am the elder."

Before Raven could reply, a sound rumbled through the wood. *Thump. Swish. Thump.* Something was coming.

"Shhh!" Thorn warned. They ducked into the shadows, scarcely daring to breathe. It seemed that every tree and boulder was suddenly fraught with peril. Then, from out of the river, there rose an enormous black beast with a long tail and two ponderous heads that swung from side to side. Its four eyes were red-hot coals.

"What is it?" Lira whispered.

"I cannot say. Never have I seen such a creature," Thorn said, "even in my most troubled dreams."

The beast emerged from the water, all its eyes seething with malice. It shook itself and lumbered straight toward the three travelers.

"Back to the tunnel!" Lira yelled. "Run!"

Thorn could not say where he found his courage. But as the beast drew closer, he was filled with unexpected calm. He fitted an arrow into his bow and took careful aim. The arrow hissed through the air and struck the beast squarely on one of its heads, then fell harmlessly to the ground.

While Thorn hurried to set another arrow, Raven raced to the water's edge and began digging out rocks with his fingers. One by one he hurled them at the raging beast, but each blow seemed only to anger it further. With a thunderous roar the creature uprooted a tree and tossed it aside as if it were merely a twig.

Hiss. Thwack. Hiss. With arrows and stones Raven and Thorn pelted the beast to no avail. Lira spied a thick branch beside the path and raised it, but the beast caught the branch in its enormous jaws and snapped it in two. Then with one massive, hairy arm it snatched Lira up and dangled her, feet first, over the rushing river.

"Thorn! Raven!" Lira yelled. "Help me!"

"*Abzecram!*" Raven shouted. "*Lorwit!*"

But the words that had so easily subdued the snarling dog had no effect at all on the angry creature. *Thump. Swish. Thump.* Determined to guard its lair, it came steadily on. Lira screamed and pounded the beast with her fists, trying to break free.

Thorn's arrows lay useless and broken beneath the creature's ponderous feet. Now all that remained was the arrow Morwid had given him. His heart pumping wildly in his chest, Thorn drew himself up and stood his ground. When the beast was no more than an arm's length away, Thorn drew back his bow and let Morwid's arrow fly.

It found its mark in the beast's chest. Stunned, the beast halted, its two heads swinging wildly to and fro. With an enraged roar it tossed Lira to the ground, then toppled dead at Thorn's feet. Wild with relief, Thorn pounded his chest and gave a mighty yell, but there was little time to celebrate his victory, for just at that moment the waters of the river receded and there emerged before the three travelers a wide path leading to the opposite shore.

"Raven!" Thorn yelled.

"I see it!" Raven cried, jubilant. "Help me with Lira."

Lira sat up, a dazed expression in her eyes. "What happened?"

"That tale must wait till we are safely across the river," Raven said.

Thorn helped his twin to her feet. "Are you hurt? Can you walk?"

Lira squared her shoulders and dusted off her breeches. "My head hurts, but I can walk."

They stepped out upon the path and, in less time than it takes to tell it, crossed the shining river.

"'Tis too late to search for Baldric," Thorn said, looking around. "We will camp here and look for him in the morning."

They cleared a campsite, beating down the under-growth, then spreading their cloaks upon it to make beds. While Lira rested, Raven busied himself making a fire with his drill and tinder. Thorn set his snare, then took the earthen vessel Morwid had given him to the river for water.

Raven set his cooking pot on the fire and boiled some comfrey leaves for Lira. "Drink this, and your sore noggin will be good as new."

Then, with their camp made and the three of them settled comfortably before the fire, the boys described for Lira Thorn's killing of the two-headed beast.

"Well done, brother!" Lira said when their tale was told. "Mother would be proud."

"Indeed," Raven said. "All of Kelhadden would be proud of your bravery."

With a courtly bow of his head Thorn accepted their praise, but his insides were still shaking. He couldn't quite understand how a single arrow had felled such a fearsome creature, nor how the death of the beast had caused the river path to open before them, bringing them to the summer country. Perhaps the spirits that had bestowed the lost amulet upon the very first king of Kelhadden were indeed helping him to get it back. Or perhaps it was Morwid's arrow that contained the magic.

Now that they were safe, Thorn was sorry he hadn't had the presence of mind to retrieve the arrow from the chest of the dead beast. Suppose there were other frightful creatures waiting in the deep forest?

Then the bushes parted and there stood the bug-eyed dwarf.

Thorn shot to his feet. "You little thief! Hand over my potion."

"Mayhap I will," the boy said, "if you be willing to strike a bargain."

"Only a fool would bargain with the likes of you." Thorn held out his hand. "Give it back."

"Oh, oh, oh. The potion. Yes indeed. I must have it here somewhere." Baldric patted the folds of his cloak, then upended his knapsack. Out tumbled a pearl bracelet, two gold rings, a half-eaten apple, a scrap of leather, and the pouch containing Thorn's dream potion.

Thorn reached for it, but Baldric snatched everything

away again and, lightning fast, shinnied up a tree. There he perched, flashing his twisted grin. "This potion must be a powerful one indeed," he cackled. "For I have chewed it, brewed it, stewed it, and yet no matter what I do, it is so hot and bitter I have not dared swallow a single drop."

Raven said, "Return it and we shall give you something far sweeter as a reward."

Lira opened her leather pouch. "I will give you a coin for it."

"'Tis not a coin I seek, but a favor. Grant it and you shall have your potion."

"I think not," Thorn declared. "You have proven you can't be trusted."

But Lira said, "Hear him out, brother, and then decide."

Thorn stepped back and tipped his face to get a better view of Baldric. "Very well," he said with a long sigh. "What do you want?"

"Nothing so dear as this potion seems to you. I wish only for safe passage to the place I seek. Nothing more."

"You are not happy here?" Lira asked.

"Happy? Look at me," Baldric said. "Everywhere I go, I am shunned, ridiculed, and worse. Though it is true I sometimes venture into the village across the river, most of my days are spent here, in the summer country, with only the birds and beasts for company." He shifted on his perch and teetered there for a moment. "By traveling high in the trees, I avoided the two-headed beast. Now he is dead, and I have you to thank for it."

"Returning my potion will be thanks aplenty," Thorn said.

But Baldric went on as if he hadn't heard. "Last spring an old woman passing through told me of a peaceful kingdom where all are welcome—young and old, rich and poor, sick and well. It is there that I wish to spend my last days, but I cannot make the journey unaided."

"Last days?" Thorn gave a short laugh. "Why, you are scarcely older than we. I wager you will live a long time yet, unless you are hanged for thieving."

"Oh, the thieving. I am not proud of it, but what choice have I? No one wants a twisted dwarf for even the meanest of tasks. We embarrass our masters and frighten small children in the street. I have thought long on it, and I am determined, before my ailing limbs grow completely useless, to seek out this secret kingdom where all live in peace."

"Methinks such a place must exist only in dreams," Raven said, "for men have enslaved and persecuted others since the dawn of time."

"I know it for a real place!" Baldric shouted with

such force that a shower of leaves fell upon the three below. "Will you take me there, in exchange for your potion?"

Lira stood beneath the tree and spoke quietly to Baldric. "I cannot blame you for seeking such a wonderful place. But we are strangers in this land and we do not know the way."

"Besides," Thorn said, "we have an important task to complete and cannot spare the time. Give me the potion, and upon our return we will help you find the place you seek."

The dwarf's face twisted. "I have no time to wait, you stupid fool! An important task, is it? You will not get far without your precious *dream* potion."

Thorn's eyes widened.

Baldric laughed. "I heard you talking in the church that night while I pretended to sleep, and though I am aught but a thief, I am smart enough to know this potion holds the key to your entire future."

Thorn feigned disinterest. "'Tis but an ordinary concoction, one easily duplicated by anyone with the simplest of training."

"You are a liar. I can see the desperation in your eyes." Baldric dangled the pouch above Thorn's head, just out of reach. "There must be others who would grant anything I asked in exchange for your potion. Yes. Yes, indeed. I shall go now and find them."

He grasped a branch and swung away through the trees.

"After him!" Raven cried.

Raven and the twins raced through the wood, but Baldric swung effortlessly from branch to branch and soon disappeared. When they grew too tired to continue the chase, Lira dropped to the ground and pressed her fingers to her temple. "We should have pretended to accept his offer and then figured out a way to outsmart him. Now he is gone, and the potion with him."

Wordlessly Thorn threw himself down beside her. Nothing had gone as he had planned. "I have learned one thing this day. I am not wise enough to be king."

Raven lay back and closed his eyes. "Not so, my friend. You have slain the beast and gained entry to the summer country."

Lira said, "You must not think too badly of yourself, Thorn. Baldric's complaint of his useless limbs clearly was a ruse. Did you not see how easily he escaped once you rejected his bargain? Why, I am certain his entire tale of the old woman and her perfect kingdom was falsehood from beginning to end. Think no more of it. Tonight I shall mix a new dream potion, and in the morning we shall be on our way to claim the amulet."

Thorn studied his twin's dirt-smudged face. Lira's braid had come undone. Her cheek was crosshatched with scratches from the brambles. A fist-size lump was forming at her temple. He wanted to tell her how grateful he was, but the words would not come. Instead he said, "Suppose Baldric finds someone willing to bargain for my potion? Suppose he dreams of the king's amulet and finds it for himself? Drucilla warned of another who would have what is rightfully mine." He stood and began to pace.

Raven rose and clasped Thorn's shoulder. "We three are clever enough to outwit the dwarf."

Lira nodded. "Why, I should not be at all surprised if we find the amulet before the morrow is through. Then we can be on our way home to Kelhadden."

Lira and Raven seemed so certain of success that hope stirred inside Thorn once more. Grateful for the fellowship of his allies, he ruffled Lira's hair and said, "Then, let us return to camp. Night comes soon."

They arrived at the camp to find their fire had gone out. While Lira rekindled it, Raven and Thorn refilled their water cups. Bone tired and ravenous after their long ordeal, they checked Thorn's snare, but it was empty. They sat around the fire waiting for the water to boil, listening to a nightingale's serenade. A thin moon shone through the trees, and the wind came up, stirring the leaves.

When the water bubbled in the pot, Lira opened her pouch and took out the herbs Raven and Thorn had taken from the garden. From the folds of her cloak she produced two small, round stones. One was a deep, coppery green; the other, nearly transparent, was the color of violets.

Thorn shot her a questioning look.

Lira placed them on his palm. "The green one is malachite, for focusing the mind. It was this very sphere that helped me cast the circle of flame the day Ranulf caught me practicing with Mother. The other is amethyst, said to aid in intuition, though it has not proven so for me yet."

Raven nodded. "With practice I am certain it will prove useful. My very own . . ." He stopped midsentence and shrugged. "No matter. Tell us your plan for making the potion."

"After I calm my thoughts with the stones, I shall try to divine how the herbs should be mixed, and boil them in the pot until the waxing of this moon. Then Thorn must drink the potion and sleep while the mixture is at its most powerful."

"Suppose I do not dream?" Thorn asked. "Or suppose I dream and cannot remember it once I wake?"

"Oh, what a worryhead!" Lira frowned at her twin. "What good is it to stew about things that may not happen at all? Cease your fretting, brother, and let me do my work."

Thorn and Raven sat quietly before the fire as Lira

held her stones, closed her eyes, and slowed her breathing.

The nightingale stopped singing and the wood went silent too, as if waiting for Lira's thoughts to settle. Sitting in the quiet clearing, Thorn felt his eyes grow heavy, for unlike the chilly air of the village they had left far behind, in the summer country it was warm and still. He was nearly asleep when Raven poked him sharply in the ribs. "Not yet!"

Lira said into the quiet, "I am ready."

With sure fingers she measured out a bit of this, a pinch of that, a palmful of the other. On its course across the heavens the moon had risen beyond the tops of the trees, heading toward its zenith. Thorn scarcely breathed as Lira tossed the herbs into the boiling water and began to speak:

> *"Boil and bubble, mystic charm,*
> *Save this prince from mortal harm.*
> *Balsam, bloodrose, light of moon,*
> *Guide him to his treasure soon."*

Using the hem of her tunic to protect her fingers from the heat of the pot, she poured the bubbling mixture into Morwid's earthen cup. "Drink this and sleep. Raven and I will keep watch."

When the concoction cooled, Thorn drank it. The

mixture was sweet on his tongue, like the brew Morwid sometimes made from honey and wildflowers to chase away a chill. Soon Thorn's head began to buzz, and the stars overhead melded into a single swirl of dazzling light. He lay down. Lira bundled her cloak and arranged it beneath her brother's head. Kneeling beside him, she placed her green and violet stones beneath his makeshift pillow.

> *"With these stones beneath your head,*
> *rest, my prince, upon your bed.*
> *'Tis a certain charm to keep*
> *witch-daughters away while you sleep."*

Almost at once Thorn fell into a deep sleep.

Raven tossed more wood on the fire and sat down next to Lira. "Witch-daughters? Though I have some experience with charms and such, I do not think I know of them."

"Nightmares," Lira said. "I want nothing to interfere with his dreams."

"Aye. What a day this has been," Raven said. "First that endless black tunnel, then the beast and that trickster Baldric. I would not say this to Thorn, for he has worries aplenty, but I fear we have not seen the last of that worrisome dwarf."

"Mayhap you are right. Still, though he be a liar and

a thief, I cannot help feeling sorry for him. It cannot be a pleasant thing to go through life despised for something you are powerless to change." Lira probed the bruised knot at her temple and stifled a yawn.

"Fighting beasts and casting charms has sapped your strength," Raven said. "You must sleep. I will keep watch."

"A tempting offer," Lira said, smiling. "But will you stay awake?"

"My tunes and my thoughts will amuse me well enough."

"You must promise to wake me in time to sleep awhile yourself," Lira said. "Good night, Raven." She touched his shoulder. "When the amulet is his and he is king, Thorn must choose a counselor. He could do no better than you."

"I'm pleased you think me worthy of such an honor, but I don't think being king's counselor is my destiny."

"Oh? Have you had some vision of your future?"

Raven was silent for several moments. In the light of the campfire his features seemed more intense than usual. Then he said, "On your solemn oath, will you keep my secret?"

"Of course."

"You know about the seer Drucilla and the child her daughter gave into safekeeping."

"Aye. Mother felt a bond with both women, for she

knows all too well the pain of giving up a child."

"I am that boy," Raven said. "My father was a member of the king's legion. My mother was not mortal, but a sea spirit who could assume human form. It's said she was born to Drucilla on the night of a great storm, and her gift was the calming of the seas."

Lira stared. "You are Drucilla's grandson?"

"Shhh! Thorn mustn't know, and you have sworn your oath."

"All right. Go on."

"Shortly after the night of the red sky, Ranulf summoned my mother and grandmother to the castle and bade them tell his future. Of course, they both claimed they could divine nothing, for they feared his wrath should their prophecies prove faulty."

"And he became enraged and threatened them with their lives," Lira said. "I can well imagine it."

"Aye. My mother feared he would harm me, though I was not long out of swaddling. She took me to a secret place deep in the forest and gave me to an old woman, another seer known for her varied gifts and her compassion. The old seer reared me as her own and attempted to pass along the secrets of her art, but beyond a few skills, like casting my voice and divining the weather, I proved an inept pupil, and she gave up."

Behind them Thorn sat up, shouted, "Away!" and promptly fell asleep again.

Lira smiled. "The potion must be working."

"Let us hope so, for Thorn must fulfill his destiny if I am to fulfill mine."

"Then, you *do* know your future!"

"It was no accident that I met Thorn on the road to the summer country that day and at about the same time you left the abbey. We both are fated to help him in his quest, but I doubt I will return to Kelhadden."

"But why? Raven, if you have had some vision, you must tell me."

Raven shrugged. "The fates may decide to intervene and change everything. But as I left the forest to find Thorn, the seer wept bitter tears as she bade me goodbye. She gave me the blessing of the dead."

"Oh! But did you not say she is quite old? Perhaps she meant that she herself would die before your return."

"I think not." Raven paused. "Forgive me if I've caused you worry, Princess."

"I can't help it! Yet you seem not to care whether you live or die."

"Of course I care, but I am half human, half spirit, and we do not think of death in the same way pure mortals do. I am willing to do anything to rid Kelhadden of the Northmen. It would be an honor to die in the service of my king, should such a sacrifice be required."

Raven got up to tend the fire. "You see why Thorn must not know these things. If he thought his quest put me in peril, he might refuse the task, or become distracted and make a fatal mistake. The forest people, few though they be, and the future of the kingdom depend upon finding that amulet. We must not allow Thorn to think of anything else. Agreed?"

"Agreed," Lira said, her mind reeling from all she had just heard. "Though I will do all in my power to keep you safe."

"Even the strongest magic cannot foil destiny," Raven said. "Let us swear an oath never to speak of these things again. And now you must sleep. On the morrow we shall learn the whereabouts of the amulet and be on our way."

Thorn tossed and turned on the hard ground. His dreams were a jumble of images of Morwid, the two-headed beast, Baldric, old March, Raven, and Lira. Toward dawn he dreamed he was struggling against a dark, cold sea and about to drown. He shouted and flailed his arms.

"Thorn! Thorn!" Dimly, through the fog of sleep, he heard Lira's voice. "Wake up!"

His whole body felt leaden, but he opened his eyes to find Raven and Lira peering anxiously into his face. He rubbed his eyes and sat up.

"Methinks that must have been some dream," Raven joked. He handed Thorn a cup of cool water. "Drink this first. Then tell us everything."

CHAPTER EIGHT

Thorn drank deeply and handed Raven the cup. "My dreams told me nothing."

Lira kicked at a loose stone and sent it tumbling into the underbrush. "My potion did not work. I've failed you, Thorn."

Thorn shrugged. Hope had deserted him as surely as a shadow on a cloudy day. "I cannot divine what the amulet is, nor where to find it. The Book of Ancients is wrong. I am not to be king."

"Perhaps you're right," Lira said, suddenly impatient with her twin. "If you're willing to give up your birthright so easily, I should find the amulet myself and rule Kelhadden as queen. Anyone worthy of the kingdom must find a way to do what must be done, even when the way is not clear."

Her words reminded Thorn of something Morwid had told him that night on the path: "Be patient and you will see your way." He said to Lira, "You're right. I can't give up. We will spend this day thinking about the amulet, and tonight I'll drink more of the potion. Perhaps then my dreams will show me where to find it."

"A wise plan," Raven said. "Now, let us see if there is something in that snare, for I am beyond hunger."

Thorn checked the snare and returned with a pheasant. Lira and Raven made a fire, and Thorn plucked the bird and fashioned a spit for roasting it. While it sizzled over the embers, Raven disappeared into the thicket and returned with a cupful of honey, which they used to sweeten their comfrey brew. After their meal Raven brought out his flute and played a sprightly tune, filling the wood with sound.

Lira sat on a stump, her face the very picture of concentration. She closed her eyes for such a long time Thorn wondered whether his twin had fallen into an enchanted sleep. But at last she said, "There may be another way to find the amulet. I wish I had remembered it sooner."

"How?" both boys asked together.

"Once, when I was very young, Mother left the castle on an urgent errand, leaving me in the care of my nurse. Though it was then the middle of December and bitterly cold, I grew restless and went out to play in the courtyard. Father's hounds were running in the yard, and one of them knocked me to the ground. I hit my head on a large stone and everything went black. The next thing I knew, my nurse was wailing loud enough to wake the dead, and I was being tended by the oldest living creature I had ever seen, an ancient being with yellowed skin and a rat's nest of white hair."

Thorn said, "An entertaining story, but I fail to see what it has to do with the amulet."

"Patience," Lira said. "I am coming to that part."

"Go ahead, Lira," Raven said.

"Well," Lira continued, obviously pleased by Raven's encouragement, "this ancient one spoke a few words in a strange language I did not understand, and almost at once the pain in my head stopped. I sat up and looked around, only to find the visitor had vanished, and Nurse and I were once again alone in the courtyard. When Mother returned that night, the nurse told her what had happened. I expected Mother to be surprised, but she merely nodded as if she had known everything all along. Then she spoke of an ancient one, part mortal, part spirit, who lives high atop an icy mountain and who, on the day of the winter solstice, grants help to whoever requests it."

"Your nurse must have sought aid from this being while you were lying there senseless," Thorn reasoned.

"But how could the ancient one know of your plight?" Raven asked. "Since your nurse obviously did not climb the mountain to seek help."

"I asked Mother that very question," Lira said. "And she promised to explain everything when I was older. Alas, soon after, we fled the castle and I never learned the answer. But now I am wondering: Suppose we find the ice mountain and inquire of this being the whereabouts of the amulet? Then we would not need the dream potion at all!"

Thorn wasn't certain this was a good idea, but he dared not voice his concerns to Lira. Like Morwid, she expected him to be wise and fearless. He didn't want to disappoint her. "I am willing to try, unless this night's dream tells me what I need to know."

"If it doesn't, we must find the ice mountain quickly," Raven said. "For the winter solstice comes soon."

In the afternoon Raven and Thorn went down to the river to fish. Lira settled herself before the fire, took out her malachite and amethyst, and tried to focus her mind. She closed her eyes and made each breath slow and even. Presently the leaves began to rustle, and behind her closed eyelids images of an owl, a hare, and a field of yellow flowers appeared. She sat quietly until the pictures settled in her mind. Then she rose, filled Thorn's earthen vessel with water, and passed her fingers over it. The water rippled and stilled. The vision came.

She glanced at the sky. Though dark clouds were gathering over the river, she collected her belongings and hurried off through the wood.

"Where can she be?" Thorn asked when the boys returned to camp with their catch.

Raven dropped their string of fish onto the ground and looked around. "I do not think she has come to harm. Perhaps she has gone exploring. Surely she will return before nightfall."

But when night came on and still Lira did not return, Thorn's uneasiness grew. "We must look for her," he said. "But where?"

"'Tis a big country," Raven said. "And Lira may yet return this night. Besides"—he broke off to perform his usual ritual for divining the weather—"we will have rain before this night is through. I am quite sure of it. Water, water everywhere!"

Rain. Water. Thorn's skin prickled, for now he remembered Drucilla's instruction, given so casually at the time, to mix the dream potion with rainwater. "That must be it!" he cried. "The potion did not work because we used water from the river. I must mix the herbs with rainwater and try again."

He was fairly dancing about the clearing in his excitement.

"Far be it from me to dampen your spirits, my friend," Raven said. "But Lira has the herbs and she is not here."

As quickly as Thorn's hopes had risen, they fell. Worse, a cold, hard suspicion wormed its way into his thoughts and lodged there. He tossed his cloak onto the ground and threw himself on it. "Truly, I am a pudding-head, Raven. For I did not suspect her at all."

"What do you mean?"

"Can you not see what has happened? Lira has gone to get the amulet for herself!" Thorn scrambled to his feet and began to pace. "Morwid warned me of another who would try to claim it. And just this morn she threatened to declare herself queen. She has the herbs for potion making. And now she has remembered the old woman on the mountain. It makes perfect sense."

"Methinks you have gotten too much sun," Raven said, "and it has addled your brain. If Lira knew where the amulet was hidden, she could have claimed it straightaway and spared herself this troublesome journey."

"She needed my help to cross the river," Thorn said. "She could not get past the two-headed beast without the help of Morwid's arrow."

Unable to think of anything that would convince

Thorn of his twin's good intentions, Raven wordlessly cleaned the fish and cooked them over the fire. But as the night wore on, neither boy felt like eating. Then the rain came, just as Raven had predicted. It lashed the forest in fitful torrents that shook the trees and sent leaves tumbling to the ground. Thorn and Raven burrowed beneath their sodden cloaks. To take his mind off his troubles, Thorn unsheathed his knife and set about making arrows, stripping new wood of its bark, trimming and shaping the points till they were sharp as bits of glass. Raven blew a few halfhearted notes on his flute, then lapsed into silence.

Presently the rain ceased, the clouds drifted by, and a sea of stars peppered the sky. The boys wrung the water from their cloaks and spread them out to dry. The fish they had cooked earlier in the evening had turned to a pasty mush, but now Thorn's stomach ached with hunger and he wolfed it down.

Raven chafed his arms. "I could do with another fire."

"Aye," Thorn said, his expression glum.

"You must not worry about Lira," Raven said. "She will return before the sun is up with some exciting story to tell. Then we shall both feel foolish for all our dithering."

Raven picked up his knapsack and a small packet fell at his feet. "By the saints!" he cried. "Lira's herbs. She did not take them after all."

"She has no need of them," Thorn said bitterly. "Her chanting and charming was a ruse."

"I do not think so. But now we have the herbs, we have the rainwater, and look! Here comes the moon. I will make a new potion. You shall dream of the amulet, and in the morning we will go and get it."

"You do not know the proper proportions."

"I watched Lira do it." Raven knelt on the ground and laid a fire with the dry shavings from Thorn's arrow making. "I am certain she used more sage than anything, for without wisdom how will you know where to look for the amulet? Next the bloodrose, for strength, and lastly a pinch of balsam, to heal whatever wounds may befall."

A spark fell onto the tinder, and he blew it till it caught, then added a few twigs. "We must try."

Thorn retrieved his earthen vessel, which had filled with rainwater during the downpour. Raven stirred the herbs into the water, and when the moon rode high in the trees, Thorn drank it down.

The nightingale took up her evening song. Raven said, "I am not as clever as Lira with charms and chants, so I shall say only, Sweet dreams, my prince, and may they prove most useful."

Thorn lay close to the fire, impatient for the potion to do its work and free him from the feeling of disappointment that threatened to overwhelm him. After wondering his whole life about his true identity, and wishing mightily for a family of his own, he knew at last who his parents were. True, Ranulf was hardly the kind of man anyone wanted for a father, but Thorn could hardly wait to see his mother. And he had found a sister, a girl who was brave, smart, and strong, and every bit as capable of ruling Kelhadden as he himself. He dreaded the struggle that would surely ensue between the two of them once the amulet was found. He tried to imagine himself standing face-to-face with Lira, his weapon drawn, ready to inflict mortal harm in order to gain the amulet, but it was impossible. How could he do battle with his twin? Harming her would be the same as harming himself.

"Thorn?" Raven said softly. "What are you muttering about?"

Thorn had not realized he'd spoken aloud. "I was thinking of Lira," he said, "but I will sleep now and dream of the amulet."

Blasted rain. Lira took refuge from the downpour in a glade beside the path. She draped her cloak over a bush to make a tent and crawled beneath it, but in no time her cloak was a sopping weight on her shoulders. She huddled in the dark, shivering. *At least I have found what I need,* she thought. *One way or the other, this quest will be over soon.*

She slowed her breath and tried to summon the hidden amulet to her mind, but the sound of raindrops plopping onto her cloak and dripping steadily from the trees made it too hard to concentrate.

Despite her discomfort, Lira was pleased with the night's work. She smiled to herself. Of course, she should have guessed Drucilla was far too clever to entrust the future of the kingdom to a potion any kitchen maid might unwittingly duplicate while seasoning a pot of soup. Sage and bloodrose had their uses, to be sure. But it was the feather of the white owl and the bone of the hare, ground fine as dust, that would make all the difference.

Though it was dark as pitch and the path through the wood was slick with mud, Lira wrapped herself in her cloak and ran.

CHAPTER NINE

IN THE MORNING THE BOYS WOKE TO BRIGHT SUN AND the soft whirr of doves' wings in the thicket. "Did the potion work?" Raven asked eagerly. "Did you dream of the amulet?"

Thorn sat up, rubbing his eyes. "I dreamed only of Morwid, and of Ranulf and his two guards. I dreamed of the sun and moon, and then my entire dream became a pure white brightness too sharp for human eyes." He frowned. "That part seemed important, but I don't know what it means. I dreamed of Lira." He glanced around the clearing. "She has not come back."

"Not yet. Mayhap she will appear in time for breakfast."

Thorn's belly was tight with hunger. "We will not wait for her. I mean to find the amulet before this day is done."

Raven was already moving about the clearing, packing up his pouch and flute and tamping down the fire.

Thorn folded his cloak and picked up his bow and quiver. "Tell me, Raven. In which direction lies the coldest clime?"

Raven clapped his hands, turned in a circle, and sniffed the sky. He pointed. "Thataway."

Thorn nodded. "Since my dreams have proven useless, we shall find the mountain of ice and look for the ancient one."

"We must leave some sign for Lira, so she will know which way we have gone."

"Let her cast a spell and find us," Thorn said, his voice thick with unshed tears. Lira had failed him. Save for Raven, he was alone in this strange country, his joy at having found his twin turned to bitter ashes. He wished he had never met her, had never known the pure happiness of finding his missing half. But he could not think now of what he had lost. There was much to be done.

They set off through the trees and walked all morning along a path that grew steeper and steeper, until at last they stood atop a hill covered with small white pebbles. In the growing chill Thorn shaded his eyes and surveyed the territory. Below lay a wide valley, and to his left, the river. To his right rose a glittering mountain, just as Lira had described it.

"If I remember rightly, the morrow marks the winter solstice," Thorn said, adjusting his heavy pack. "If Lira's story is true, the ancient one on the mountain will help me find the amulet."

"The mountain looks slippery as glass," Raven said, squinting into the sun. "Can you climb it?"

For the first time in a very long while Thorn felt himself smiling. "Old Morwid taught me. I have spent all my life climbing the cliffs near the sea cave. When I was very small, he called me *haedus,* 'little goat'—for I am quick and sure-footed."

"Come along, then, little goat," Raven said, clapping his friend on the shoulder. "If the weather holds, we will reach the mountain before nightfall."

Lira stood in the middle of an alder grove, trying not to panic. Nothing looked familiar. On her way out of camp the previous day she had passed a tumbling brook and a meadow filled with yellow flowers, but here there was nothing but brown stubble and a path leading ever downward toward a shadowed vale. As she made her way along the trail, the wind soughed in the trees. And then she heard the noisy intake of human breath. She stopped to listen, but nothing stirred. On she went.

Soon another sound, like a long exhalation of air, was followed by an anguished wail. Deep, sorrowful moans followed one after the other, filling the valley with mournful sound. The hairs on her neck stood up. "The Valley of Sighs!" she said aloud. "But which way leads out of this desolate place?"

"You do not like my little valley?"

Lira spun around. The voice, familiar to her now, came from somewhere above. She craned her neck and peered into the trees. "Baldric!"

"One and the same!" He skittered out to the edge of the tree branch and cackled. "The Valley of Sighs, oh yes indeed. Not a very happy place. But soon I will be on my way to the peaceful kingdom."

Though certain she now possessed the missing ingredients for making the dream potion herself, Lira very much wanted to have Drucilla's mixture back. Reaching into her pouch, she brought out a wilted bloom she had picked the day before and held it out to Baldric. "Remember how bitter the potion was, no matter how you chewed it, brewed it, or stewed it?"

He merely fixed her with a bug-eyed stare.

"Well," Lira went on, "this flower is the missing ingredient that must be added in just the right proportion to sweeten the brew. I do not think you will find anyone interested in an incomplete mixture. Give me the potion and I will fix it."

He laughed. "'Tis only my limbs that are twisted, not my brain, you fool! Why should I trust you?"

"My brother and I had a terrible fight," Lira said, hoping her words sounded truthful. "Whether he recovers his potion or not is of no concern to me."

"Oh my, oh my, oh my." Baldric shook his head and made a tsk-tsking sound. "A family squabble, was it? What a shame. However, I have no need of your skills now, girl, for I know that flower. 'Tis common as fleas."

"But you do not know how much to add, nor how to prepare it. Too much, or too little, added in the wrong way will produce the direst of consequences."

"In this valley there must be at least one who is trained in your art. I will find someone to complete the potion. And so, here I go. Turrah!"

With a gleeful chortle Baldric swung away through the trees.

Blast that little thief! Lira stared after him, hoping his goose chase would buy the time she needed. Wondering which way to go, she took out her amethyst, sat on the ground, and closed her eyes. "South or north, west or east, winds of doubt shall be now ceased. North or south, east or west, which way out will be the best?"

Lira opened her eyes. In the distance there appeared a majestic mountain, glistening like crystal. A white owl appeared, hooting and circling above her head. She picked up her pouch and hurried after it.

By midafternoon the air had turned bitterly cold. Eager to reach the base of the mountain before nightfall, Thorn pushed ahead through the fading light, till the snow came down upon them in a thick, blinding swirl and Raven said, "Enough."

They made a fire and huddled inside their cloaks, too exhausted to set a snare. Raven took a handful of berries from his pouch and passed half of them to Thorn.

"I am worried about Lira," Raven confessed, wiping berry juice from his chin. "Something has happened, else she would have caught up with us by now."

"I fear she has no intention of finding us." Thorn munched on the berries and fought the sorrow and hurt building inside him. He didn't want to think Lira actually meant to find the amulet and claim Kelhadden for her own, but what else could explain her sudden absence? He sighed. "Whether my twin is friend or foe I can't say, but I cannot dwell upon it. I must find the amulet."

"A wise ruler thinks first of the greatest good, even at the expense of his own heart," Raven agreed. "Still, it would be too bad to lose your twin so soon after finding her."

"Aye." Despite his best efforts not to cry, tears welled in Thorn's eyes. Since meeting Lira, he had begun to dream of the day they would go home to Kelhadden. He planned to teach her all he had learned during his years in Morwid's cave. He hoped she would teach him how to ride a horse and how to cast a circle of flame. Perhaps he would get his flute from the cave and together they would make the castle walls ring with music once again.

"You must not be hasty in your judgments," Raven said. "Lira may yet prove herself a true friend, and a great help to you when you are king."

Thorn studied his companion. Raven's dark hair curled damply over his narrow forehead, giving him the look of a playful imp, but his expression was quite serious.

Thorn tossed a twig on the fire. "It is you I want for counselor, for you have proven wise and true."

"'Tis too early to speak of such things," Raven said. "Methinks—"

"Shhh!" Thorn grabbed Raven's arm. "Footsteps."

"Who goes there?" Thorn called.

When there was no answer, Thorn grabbed a branch from the fire and held it aloft like a torch. "Who is it?"

"Who is it? Who is it? Who is it?" came a voice from the darkness.

"Baldric!" Raven cried.

"One and the same!" With a rollicking laugh the trickster shuffled into the circle of firelight.

"What do you want this time?" Thorn tossed the branch onto the fire.

"What do I want? I want what everyone wants. A warm fire, a full belly, and the companionship of true friends. But the last seems always to elude us, does it not? Why, just this morn I met your twin and learned that you had gone your separate ways. So sad."

"What do you mean?" Thorn asked.

Baldric shrugged. "It seems she wants the potion for herself, but she will not succeed unless she shows more cleverness than she did this day." He stood warming his hands before the fire as if he had been invited. "She tried to get it back by saying it needed the addition of a certain flower, but then she had no more sense than to show me which bloom! Stupid girl!" He opened his cloak and a shower of yellow flowers tumbled onto the snow. "Common as weeds."

Thorn picked one up and sniffed it. The musty smell reminded him of home and the Book of Ancients. He turned the flower over in his hand, studying the compact petals, wondering whether this truly was the missing part of the dream potion or merely another of Baldric's lies.

While Baldric was gloating over his own cleverness, Raven quietly rose from the fire and took a length of rope from his knapsack. Thorn saw that his companion meant to capture Baldric.

To distract the interloper, Thorn said, "Where is Lira? Did she say where she would go?"

One silent step at a time Raven crept closer to Baldric.

"I left your twin in the Valley of Sighs, but she is clever enough to find her way—oompf!"

Thorn lunged at the boy and sent him tumbling onto the ground. Raven bent over Baldric and quickly bound his wrists.

"Let me up, you fool!" Baldric sputtered. "How dare you?"

"How dare *you* steal what is rightfully mine?" Thorn hauled Baldric to his feet and began turning him in a tight circle as Raven wound the rope around and around his body.

"Oh, oh, oh," cried Baldric. "Look at how cruelly he treats the weak and afflicted!"

Thorn's eyes shone with merriment. "The weak and afflicted, Baldric? *You?*"

Raven made fast the knot and patted Baldric's shoulder. "There. Methinks that will hold you till you decide to return the dream potion."

"Never!" Baldric shouted, growing red faced as he twisted this way and that.

"As you wish," Thorn said, settling himself before the fire again.

Raven took out his flute. "Shall I play you a tune, Baldric?"

Though Baldric's furious stare was his only answer, Raven blew a series of notes so pure Thorn thought surely his companion's flute must possess some kind of enchantment. And indeed, after a while Baldric drifted into sleep.

Thorn knelt in the snow beside the dwarf, searching for the stolen dream potion. If he could find Drucilla's original mixture, he would try once more to dream of the amulet and perhaps avoid the arduous climb up the foreboding mountain.

But the potion was not to be found in the folds of Baldric's cloak, nor in his knapsack, nor in the pouch he wore around his neck.

"He must have hidden it somewhere," Thorn whispered to Raven.

"Or made someone a bargain for it."

"Mayhap Lira has it and is at this moment on her way to claim the amulet."

Raven scratched his head. "'Tis a puzzle, true enough. But here is what I propose: We still have some water from last night's rain. Let us mix the yellow flower with the potion Lira made and see if it improves upon your dream."

"It's worth a try." Thorn looked up at the sheer wall of shimmering ice so tall it seemed to pierce the clouds. Anything that might spare him the ordeal of the long climb seemed worth doing. But he was, after all, the prince; if the potion did not work, he would not shirk his duty. He must do whatever was required to find the amulet and return it to Kelhadden.

Thorn set the pot on the fire, and when the water bubbled, Raven mixed a handful of the strange yellow petals with pinches of sage, balsam, and bloodrose and dumped the concoction into the water. When it had cooled, Thorn drank it down and wrapped himself in his cloak.

"Sweet dreams," Raven whispered. "I shall play you a soothing tune whilst you sleep."

Though in truth the music was sweet, Thorn's dreams were bitter as tansy. In his mind's eye he witnessed everything bad that had happened in the world, blood-chilling cruelty and deceit, greed and murder, starvation and death, and then he glimpsed the future in all its terror and beauty, and woke in a drenching sweat despite the frigid night air.

"What happened?" Raven asked. "A visit from the witch-daughters? You are shivering, and I don't think it's from the cold."

But Thorn could not speak of his harrowing dream, which even now seemed much too real. "I did not learn anything useful," he said, wiping the sweat from his brow, "except that the potion we made last night is far too strong for mortals." He rose and gathered his bow and the new arrows he had made. "'Tis nearly dawn and my belly is empty. Perhaps a hunt will calm my mind."

"Wait!" Baldric shouted. "Untie me, you fools, before I piss all over myself. It has been a long night in these ropes."

"Give us the potion first," Thorn said.

"I do not have it," Baldric said, desperation crowding his voice.

"But I wager you can tell us where to find it," Raven said. He picked up the water pot and Thorn's cup and began pouring water, ever so slowly, from one container to the other. *Drip. Drip. Drip.*

Baldric's eyes bulged even more. "Oh, what torture! Stop! Stop and I will tell you where to find it."

"Speak quickly, then," Thorn said, his breath clouding the air. "For the sun is nearly up, and I cannot waste a single hour of this day."

"In the elm grove near your first camp," Baldric said on a rush of breath, "you will find a pile of stones in the shape of a cross. The potion is hidden there beneath the stones. I will take you there myself, I swear it. Now, I beg you, untie me, before it is too late!"

Raven worked the knots free, and in a trice the dwarf disappeared.

"After him!" Raven cried.

But Thorn merely slung his quiver over his shoulder. "That little thief had no intention of leading us to the potion."

"Should we not go and get it before he moves it again?" Raven asked.

"It isn't there. Think, Raven. All around our camp were dozens and dozens of oak trees, and not one elm to be found anywhere. No doubt Baldric meant to send us on some merry chase. I am through with dreams and spells and potions."

Filled with new determination, Thorn drew himself up. "I will scale the mountain as planned. If the ancient one will not help me find the amulet, I will look elsewhere. I will not go back to Kelhadden without it."

So saying, he entered the snowy wood and presently returned with a hare, which he and Raven cleaned and roasted with dispatch. Then, their hunger satisfied, they set off for the mountain.

❧ CHAPTER TEN ❧

A MORNING'S WALK BROUGHT THEM TO THE BASE OF THE mountain. Raven looked up at the craggy spire and whistled under his breath. "It *is* made of ice! How will you climb it?"

Thorn was already busy sorting through the contents of his pack. "I am certain Morwid gave me everything I need."

Raven took out his drill and tinder and set about making a fire. Thorn left his pack and walked along the base of the mountain, studying the surface from every angle. In places where the ice was thickest, the cliff was blackened and rough with frozen pebbles. But where the ice was transparent he could see deep holes in the rock, as if a giant had gouged them with his fingers. Here and there were narrow outcroppings that would serve as footholds if he could break though the ice.

As he stood there, Morwid's voice came to him as clearly as if the old man himself were whispering into his ear: "You must walk the frozen pools and scale the icy mountain's soaring tops . . . the blade of your knife tempered by fire . . ."

Thorn hurried back to Raven. "I need the rope you used for binding Baldric."

"Of course you are welcome to it," Raven said, "but I do not think it is long enough to be of much use."

With his knife Thorn raked hot coals from the fire into his earthen bowl, then wrapped the bowl in his cloak and tied it about his waist.

Raven scratched his head. "Dare I ask why you wear a bowl of hot coals strapped about your middle?"

"I will heat my knife with these coals and melt the ice that fills the crannies. Then I can make my way up the mountain."

Raven craned his neck and squinted at the narrow peak. "'Tis a long way to the top. Still, your plan might succeed if the coals do not burn too fast."

"I will take more tinder to keep them burning."

"I will wait for you here."

"If I do not return—"

Raven stopped Thorn with an upraised palm. "You will come back. Is there anything else you need?"

"Aye. Plenty of courage and more than a little good fortune."

Together the boys walked along the base of the mountain until they came to a place where the ice was thin and clear. Thorn held the blade of his dirk in the coals and, when it was hot, touched it to the ice. The ice melted. A trickle of water ran down the mountain face. Thorn chipped away at the thinned edge until the ice cracked and, with a light tinkling sound, slid to the ground. While Raven supplied tinder for the coals, Thorn worked his way up the face of the mountain, melting the ice and chipping it away. When he could no longer reach the crannies from the ground, he stood on Raven's shoulders and made places for his feet and hands.

"Is there no faster way to climb this mountain?" Raven asked.

"If you have a better plan, let us hear it," Thorn muttered, for he, too, was discouraged by having to work at a snail's pace.

But Raven shook his head. "I cannot think of another way."

"Then I must begin."

Raven unclasped his cloak and offered it to Thorn. "You will be cold once the sun sets."

"So will you."

"I will warm myself by the fire," Raven said, "and keep it burning until you come back."

With that, Thorn fastened the cloak around his shoulders, fitted his foot into a newly freed hole in the rock, and began to climb.

Raven gathered more wood for the fire and huddled before the flames, watching Thorn's slow progress up the mountain. Now and then he heard the faint crack of breaking ice and the ring of Thorn's blade on stone. He stayed awake far into the night, straining his ears for any sound that meant Thorn was still safe, still climbing. But at last the sounds stilled, and he fell asleep.

"Raven! Wake up!"

Raven jerked awake and peered through the swirling fog that had developed in the night. A bleary-eyed and bedraggled Lira plopped herself down before the fire.

"Lira! Where have you been?" Raven demanded. "Thorn thinks you mean to use your gifts to get the amulet and claim Kelhadden for yourself."

"By all the saints in heaven!" Lira said. "Does he think I am no better than that thief Baldric, even after all I have done to help him?" She picked up a stick of firewood and pounded the glowing coals until a shower of orange sparks spiraled into the darkness. "I *would* make an excellent queen, if I say so myself. But I wouldn't rob my twin of his birthright." She looked around. "Where is he?"

Raven yawned and pointed. "On the mountain. He is through with chants and potions." Raven explained Thorn's method for scaling the slick peak.

"Then, all my trouble is for naught," Lira said. "After Thorn could not dream, I tried to divine the reason my potion did not work. In a vision I saw what was missing and went in search of it, but I got lost in the storm and wound up in the Valley of Sighs."

"Where Baldric found you," Raven finished. "He was here only yesterday with some tale of a yellow flower."

"I picked it merely for its beauty," Lira said. "I told him it was the missing part of Drucilla's dream potion in hopes of tricking him into giving it back, but he is too clever for me."

"He is a cunning creature," Raven agreed. "But let us waste no more thought on that trickster. We must help Thorn find the amulet."

"God's elbows!" Lira cried. "That is what I have been *trying* to do since first I set eyes upon him."

"Weariness has made you cross," Raven said mildly. He took out the last of yesterday's roasted hare and handed it to her. "I meant to save this for Thorn, but you need it worse."

"Bless you, Raven! I am too hungry for words."

Lira wasted no time in devouring Raven's offering. When she finished, they piled more wood onto the fire and settled in to wait.

Thorn rose from the narrow outcropping where he had passed a sleepless night tending his coals, and studied the mass of rock looming before him. To his right was another narrow ledge, and past the ledge, leading upward, lay a series of deep crevices slick with ice. Standing above the layer of fog blanketing the hills and valleys, he watched sunlight creeping across the face of the mountain, flooding the creases and crannies with a radiance that turned everything to gold.

He rubbed the cramps from his legs, fastened his bowl of fire around his waist, and inched his way onto the next ledge. One foot slipped as he hit a pile of stones that had formed in a fissure in the rock. He stumbled, his arms waving wildly. But then he righted himself and stood hugging the mountain till his breathing slowed. When his hands steadied, he touched the tip of his knife to the coals, then chipped away at the ice, not thinking past the next handhold that would bring him closer to the amulet.

Suppose I do not find the amulet? Suppose the ancient one refuses to help me? The questions buzzed like pesky mosquitoes in Thorn's ear, and he shook his head as if to dislodge them. The ice cracked at last. Thorn fitted his hands and feet into the shallow depressions and hauled himself up again. As the morning wore on, he fell into a rhythm of heating the dirk, chipping the melting ice, and climbing. He kept a sharp eye on the coals, tipping out the ash and adding just enough tinder to keep the fire hot.

Near midday he drew himself onto yet another ledge and stopped to regain his breath. Just as his feet found purchase on the rocky outcropping, a deep rumble began from somewhere inside the mountain, and it began to quake. The ledge cracked. The pebbles beneath his feet shook and rolled away. Stones and boulders rained down. Thorn dodged the tumbling rocks, his fingers digging into cracks and crannies, certain that in the next moment he would lose his grip and fall to his death. He clung to the mountain, his breath coming in short, painful gasps as the boulders crashed onto the ledge, then bounced off and tumbled to the ground far below.

As suddenly as the rumbling had begun, it stopped. Thorn looked up, surprised to see that he was near the mountaintop. Once more he heated the blade of his knife, and once more he dug into the ice, making places for his hands and feet. With a final heave he scrambled up and stood on the peak, shivering and exhausted.

At first he saw nothing but more boulders and a few

patches of gray green moss, but then he heard a noise behind him and he whirled around. "Oh!"

His knees buckled. He went numb. Right in front of him on a giant toadstool sat a creature so strange Thorn was not certain whether it was mortal or spirit.

"Ah," said the creature in a voice that reminded Thorn of a creaky wagon wheel. "You have come at last, Thorn. And not a moment too soon."

Thorn saw now that the creature was a wizened woman with custard-yellow skin and a wild halo of thick white hair. She wore a shapeless cloak and, around her wrist, a bracelet fashioned from purple thistle.

In a voice tinged with wonder Thorn said, "You know me!"

The ancient being said nothing, but merely held his wondering gaze.

"If you know who I am, then you must know I have come for the king's lost amulet," Thorn said at last.

"I know why you have come, but finding the amulet will not be so easy."

"Easy?" Thorn cried. "I have fought my way through the ice with hot coals strapped about my waist, and dodged a storm of tumbling boulders heavy enough to slay a giant! My hands are raw with blisters. I have had neither food nor sleep since beginning this climb. And now I must turn around and make my way down again." He paused to catch his breath. Then, remembering he had come to beg a favor, he went on more calmly, "It is said that on the winter solstice you will give aid to whoever asks for it. If it please you, will you give the amulet into my care? Kelhadden is sorely in need of it."

The ancient one rose from the toadstool, and the smell of old flowers wafted up. "It *would* please me, much more than you know, to give you that which you seek, but even I am powerless to hand over something as important as the amulet. Still, there is something I can do." She turned and said over her shoulder, "Come with me."

Thorn left his belongings and followed the woman down a narrow stone path and into a dim cave that smelled of spice and secrets. Once inside he blinked and looked around. Stone jars were piled willy-nilly against one wall. A stack of dusty leather-bound books, their spines cracked with age, littered a table. Sundials, wooden casks, a cracked looking glass, and a broken spinning wheel spilled from the corners. A red-eyed lizard streaked across the dirt floor, leapt onto a stone jar, and perched on the old woman's shoulder. "There, there," she crooned. "No need to fear this one."

She smiled at Thorn. "We do not get many visitors here, you see." A bit of dried seaweed fell from a basket suspended from the ceiling and landed in her hair, but she took no note of it. With the lizard riding her shoulder, she bent to a trunk and took out a leather doublet worn soft with age. Then she sat cross-legged on the floor and motioned for Thorn to join her. When they were seated face-to-face, she closed her eyes and chanted:

> *"Tested once, tested twice,*
> *this noble prince is tested thrice*
> *by raging wind, by fire and ice.*
> *Spirits of the sea and glade,*
> *who round his head your magic made,*
> *guard him well through lake and glen*
> *and see him safely home again."*

The ancient one opened her eyes. "An evening's walk east from the base of this mountain will bring you to the Cave of the Wind. Inside you will find a rune stone that will lead you to the amulet. The cave is a frightful place, though no more so than the Lake of Fire. Wear this doublet inside out as a charm against the terrors yet to come."

"Lake of Fire?" Thorn's voice shook as he slipped the doublet over his tunic.

"I would spare you that ordeal if I could, but we must trust the wisdom of the spirits and your own courage to see you through." The old woman paused. "Your belief in yourself will enable you to do what you must."

As they left the cave and returned up the path, the ancient one said, "You must act quickly. You have but two days to find the amulet, for there is another who would have it."

"Aye," Thorn said, "my very own sister, whom I once counted as a friend."

"Fortune makes friends, and adversity tries them. That is all I have to say."

Then, quick and quiet as a wisp of smoke, the old woman vanished.

Thorn stared first at the empty toadstool, then at the doublet that came nearly to his ankles, wondering whether he was caught up in a dream that would dissolve with the lighting of a torch. But on the ground beside the toadstool lay his dirk, his bowl of glowing coals, and Raven's cloak, just where he had left them. Shading his eyes, he peered into the valley far below. Beneath an azure sky the vale led away to a great stone wall that seemed to have no beginning and no end. Just above his head small yellow birds and a cloud of silver butterflies danced in the light. He stood still, as if enchanted, so entranced that for a moment he forgot why he had come.

Then he felt an insistent aching deep in his bones, and his bloodied hands began to throb. His throat closed up and his eyes stung. After everything he had already endured, a frightful cave and a fiery lake still stood between him and the amulet. Overcome with despair, he flung himself onto the ground. "I am finished! I cannot do it."

He buried his head in his arms and sobbed until his insides were raw.

Morwid, he thought. *Tell me what to do.* Yet he realized he had embarked upon this quest as much for his own reasons as to save the kingdom and avenge Morwid. He wanted to know more about who he was, where he had come from, and what he could do. Now the answers were unfolding before him, and finding the amulet was proving harder than he'd ever imagined. If he was to succeed, he needed to master his fear and overcome his pain. He sat up and wiped his eyes, watching the shadows lengthening along the face of the cliffs. Soon darkness would come. Thorn gathered his belongings and started down the mountain.

The sun had kept his handholds free of ice, and now that he knew where the crevices and ledges were, the return went quickly, so that Thorn found himself near the base of the mountain when darkness came. He dared not stop to rest. Time was running out.

"Thorn!"

"Raven?" he shouted, peering into the darkness below.

"'Tis Lira! Hurry and come down."

"You may as well go away," he yelled, "for I do not have the king's amulet."

"You will have it soon!" Lira shouted back. "I know how to make the dream potion work."

Another few steps found Thorn off the mountain and standing face-to-face with his twin. "I do not need your dream potion," he said coldly, "for I know how to find the amulet. Even if I did not, I would not trust you." He pushed past her. "Where is Raven?"

"Roasting a hare for your supper." Lira matched her strides to her twin's. "We watched your progress down the mountain all afternoon and hoped to make you a pleasant meal, but we did not count on finding you in such a foul temper. And I think it's most unkind of you to say you cannot trust me, when I have spent the last two days trying to help you find that blasted amulet!"

"To help yourself to it, you mean," Thorn said. "Baldric said so."

"Baldric? You would trust the word of a witless thief rather than that of your own twin?" Lira let out an exasperated sigh. "I told Baldric that you and I had fought, hoping he would think we were enemies and give me Drucilla's potion. I failed, but now I hardly care! I'm tired of risking life and limb to help you when you are too thick-headed to appreciate it!"

Before Thorn could reply, Raven appeared. "You are safe," he said, "but what of the amulet? And where did you get that doublet? Do you realize you have put it on wrong side out?"

"I will tell you everything," Thorn said, "but we must hurry." Turning to his twin, he continued, "Forgive me, sister. When you left our camp without a word and did not return, I thought the worst. I misjudged you."

"Think twice next time! Jumping to conclusions is not a wise habit in a king," Lira said. "If you want my help, you must trust me."

"I know that now," Thorn said as they approached the fire. "One thing still puzzles me, though. If it is not you who will challenge me for the amulet, who will?"

"Time to think on that later," Raven said. "Come. The hare is nearly done. Tell us what happened on the mountain, and then I will make a merry tune to wash away our cares."

While they ate their supper, Thorn described his encounter with the strange creature on the mountain and her gift of the leather doublet. "We have but two days to find the amulet," he said. "And after the cave I must swim a lake of fire to find it."

"Why, you are fairly trembling!" Lira said. "Are you still cold, despite this fine fire?"

Thorn said, "Morwid once told me our grandfather lost the kingdom because he did not wish to be thought weak and afraid." He paused. "I *am* weak and afraid, which is far worse."

"You are not weak," Lira said. "You killed the beast

and climbed a mountain of ice. Besides, I think it's wise to heed our fears, for sometimes fears can save us. Tell me, what frightens you so?"

Her kindly expression made it easy for Thorn to confess. "All my life I have lived in mortal dread of swimming, and I do not know why." He tossed a bone into the fire. "It shames me, Lira. The people must not have a coward for a king."

Raven blew a sweet melody on his flute. Lira stared into the flames. "I wonder . . ." she began. "Many years ago, when Mother and I still lived in the castle, I would beg her to tell the story of the night you and I were born. I never tired of hearing about the red sky and the clever way Mother sent you to safety, though it proved a near disaster. Mother told me the maid, in her haste to deliver you into Morwid's safekeeping, lost her footing on the rocks and fell headfirst into the sea! Both of you were nearly drowned."

"'Tis surprising the maid would admit to such carelessness," Raven said before beginning another song.

"Oh, she did not admit it, at least to Mother. She told the dairymaid, the dairymaid told the stable boy, the stable boy told the chambermaid, and the *chambermaid* told Mother."

Remembering the vaguely familiar terror that seized him during his first swimming lesson with Morwid, Thorn said, "It *must* be the memory of that night that makes me afraid. Morwid often told of how he found me outside his cave, damp and shivering."

"All that is past," Lira said. "You must think now of the future."

Nearly sick with shame at having so thoroughly misjudged his twin, Thorn said to her, "Someday I will find a way to repay your kindness."

"When the Northmen are vanquished and our kingdom is restored, that will be thanks enough," Lira said.

The moon rose through the dark trees. Though he was bone weary and sore, Thorn dared not stop to rest. He rose. Lira placed her hands on his shoulders, and their eyes met. *Believe in yourself.*

Hearing her thought as clearly as if she had spoken aloud, Thorn nodded. "Gather your packs," he said to his companions. "We must find the cave."

CHAPTER ELEVEN

In the cold moonlight they hastened along a trail overgrown with thorny bushes and sharp brown grasses that waved like spears in the wind. With Thorn in the lead, the three travelers raced over patches of hardened snow and through thickets of briers that scratched their faces and tore at their cloaks. On and on they ran until, at the rising of the sun, the mouth of the cave loomed ahead, dark and forbidding.

Thorn strode to the entrance and peered into the blackness. "I do not think it's wise for all of us to venture inside. I will go alone."

"But—" Lira began.

"When I have found the rune stone, we will seek the

lake together." Placing both hands on Lira's shoulders, he said, "I regret that I ever doubted your intentions. If I do not come back—"

"Do not speak of such things!"

"If I do not come back, claim the amulet in my name and rid our homeland of the Northmen. Rule in my stead, with Raven as your counselor."

"'Tis not my destiny to . . ." Raven began, then stopped himself. "Have you your pouch and quiver, your arrows and your dirk?"

"Aye. And the rest of Morwid's gifts."

"Wait while I make a torch to light your path," Raven said.

But Thorn shook his head. "I have but hours to find the amulet. Besides, I was reared in a cave. I can find my way."

"All the same," Lira said, rummaging in her pouch, "take this."

She handed him a smooth, round stone of deepest blue. "'Tis a sending stone. If you run into trouble, hold it tightly and send me your thoughts. I will do all I can to help you."

With a quick wave Thorn stepped inside the cave. Soon he was swallowed in blackness. When his eyes adjusted to the dark, he could see a few slivers of light poking through chinks in the stone walls, and dark circles on the floor where water had recently stood. This cave did not seem all that different from Morwid's, or from those he had explored while training with the old warrior. Feeling his way along one wall, Thorn realized the cave held many tunnels leading in different directions. Which one would take him to the rune stone and out the other side?

His heart thrummed in his chest. A wrong decision might well bring disaster, and there was no time to waste. He chose a tunnel and edged his way along the slick, hard floor. Above him came a steady *drip, drip* of water on stone.

He could not say how long he followed the tunnel, straining his eyes in the darkness, but after a while his foot bumped a solid wall in front of him.

"Blast!" he muttered. "A dead end!" He turned around and retraced his steps, arriving after some time at the place where he had begun. *I must not lose my way again.* He fumbled in his pouch for the ball of twine Morwid had given him and let it play out behind him, marking his trail as he started down another dark tunnel.

Soon he entered a maze of small, tight spaces where the air was close and hot. Thin shards of light slanted through the crevices above him. Something rattled beneath his feet. He peered into the darkness. Bones!

Surely they were the remains of Northmen who had

failed in their quest for the amulet. Beside the piles of bones and mummified bodies lay shields, dirks, and a broken broadsword. Thorn's stomach churned. Suppose he, too, became lost in the cave forever? Sweat chilled his forehead and stung his eyes as he crawled in and out of one dark space after another.

Then a fearsome, howling wind began, a yowling, screeching racket that pierced his eardrums as surely as a huntsman's arrow. He screamed and clawed at the walls, his ears bursting with the sound. His body was seized with a violent trembling. He scurried frantically down one narrow tunnel, then another. The ball of twine slipped from his grasp and rolled away into the dark. The shrieking wind pounded in his brain. He was drenched in sweat, drained of all his resources. Alone in the terrible blackness.

Bereft of hope, he forced himself to take another step. And they were upon him. A solid black horde of stealthy rats, clawing and screeching, filling his mouth and burrowing into his ears. The entire cave seemed alive with them. They crawled into his hair, clung to his leather doublet, and hung there as he tried to flee. Sharp teeth pierced his skin. Blood trickled down his face. He grabbed the rats one by one and tossed them away, but more, and still more, descended on him, their bodies soft and squishy beneath his boots as he fought to free himself. His fingers closed over the sending stone. *Lira. Help me!* He took a running leap, and then he was falling through nothingness, down, down through the darkness.

Outside the cave Raven and Lira grew ever more restless as the day wore on with no sign of Thorn. Glancing at the sky, Raven said, "By this time on the morrow either Thorn will have the amulet, or his rival will."

"Aye." For the first time since meeting her twin, Lira began to doubt the outcome of his quest. "Perhaps the Book of Ancients is wrong and the Northmen will rule Kelhadden forever. Then I shall never see my mother again."

"You must not lose hope," Raven said. "The fates would not bring Thorn this far only to let him fail."

Just then Lira was overcome with such a piercing pain in her ears that she covered them with her palms and fell to her knees, tears pouring from her eyes. Raven bent over her. "What is the matter?"

"Thorn!" she gasped. "He is in trouble."

Raven wheeled and snatched up his drill and tinder. "We'll make a torch and go after him."

By the time the fire caught, Lira's pain had eased. She ripped her cloak into long strips and bound them to a stick. Raven banked the fire, jammed his feathered hat on his head, and picked up his pouch. "Ready?"

Lira touched her branch to the flame. The cloth

strips smoldered and caught. She and Raven entered the cave, Raven holding the torch high as they surveyed the narrow space. In the dank, cobwebbed tunnel, twisting shadows danced on the walls.

"Which way?" Lira asked.

"There." Raven knelt on the floor of the cave. "Thorn's twine."

They followed the trail through one twisting tunnel and out the next until their torch burned low and the trail of twine abruptly ended.

"Now what?" Lira asked.

"We have but little fire left," Raven said just as the tortured shrieking of the wind reached their ears.

"We must find Thorn!" Lira yelled, and clapped her palms over her ears to muffle the sound, her eyes darting frantically about the cave. "He must be here!"

"Thorn!" they shouted above the noise of the wind. "Thorn!"

Then the horde of rats dropped from the ceiling and into Lira's hair. She screamed and tried to bat them away as they crawled into her ears and burrowed beneath her tunic. "Raven! Help me!"

Raven fought off the rats clinging to his own tunic and waved his burning torch about the cave. "*Abzecram! Lorwit!*"

The screeching ceased. The rats scurried away into the deep recesses of the cave.

"Are you all right?" Raven asked. "You're trembling."

"I think so." Lira shuddered and raked her hair from her eyes. "There is nothing in this world I hate more than rats!"

"Come on," Raven said. "We must find Thorn."

They jumped across a narrow schism. Lira peered into the blackness and saw a faint glimmer of light. "Look! Down there!"

She grasped Raven's hand and they slid feetfirst down a long tunnel, where they found Thorn lying on a patch of moss. In his hand was Morwid's mirror, reflecting the torchlight.

Raven cast aside his dying torch. It rolled away and landed against a boulder with a loud *thump*. And then a door opened right in front of them. The howling wind abruptly ceased. Through the open passageway Lira glimpsed sunlight, brown grass, and a glorious patch of blue sky.

Torn between laughter and tears, she shouldered Thorn's quiver and pouch and helped Raven pull her twin out of the tunnel. "Thorn!" she cried. "Wake up!"

But Thorn didn't move.

"Balsam," she said to Raven. "Quickly! And bloodrose if there be any left."

Raven opened his pack and took out the herbs. "We have no water for brewing them."

Taking up a small stone, Lira ground the herbs into her palm and placed them on her brother's tongue. She knelt beside him in the dirt and with her sleeve wiped the blood from his brow.

Raven, his thin face streaked with sweat and dust, bent over his prince. "You have come so far," he whispered. "Don't abandon your quest now. Everything depends upon these next hours."

"We must have water for a healing potion," Lira said, her voice breaking.

"Aye. Will you be all right till I return?"

She nodded.

Raven picked up his pouch. "If he wakes in the meantime, you must go on without me."

"But—"

"The day wanes, and time will not stop, even for a prince. Promise you will go, and I will catch up as soon as I can."

"All right. But hurry!"

When Raven had gone, Lira settled herself beside her twin. To keep her mounting fear at bay, she began to prattle. "Shall I tell you a story about our mother, Thorn? When I was very small, after my bath and supper, my nurse would take me upstairs to see Mother in her bedchamber. Often I would find her standing at the window, her embroidery forgotten in her hand, gazing out at the sky as if waiting for something wonderful to happen. She must have been thinking of you and waiting for the day you would claim Kelhadden.

"Other nights she would be in her bed with her coverlets drawn about her shoulders, looking for all the world like a beautiful swan nestled in a pillow of lace. Of course, if our father was home, I couldn't stay, but when he was away, I would climb into her bed and she would make rhymes for me till I fell asleep."

Thorn gave no sign of having heard her. Lira bent closer and gave his arm a hard shake. "Unless you wake, Ranulf will go on stealing and killing and starving the forest people, including our mother. I'm certain you would not wish such a life for anyone."

She paused, hoping for some reply, but Thorn lay still. Fighting her tears, Lira went on. "I know what I said about ruling Kelhadden myself, and I can do it if need be, but I wish you would wake up, Thorn."

"So many words!" Thorn muttered. He blinked and sat up, shading his eyes against the light.

"I thought you would never wake," Lira said with a shaky breath. "Are you all right?"

"How did I get here?" He stuck out his tongue and with his fingers removed bits of the dried herbs, then spat.

"I heard your cry for help through the sending stone. We found you at the bottom of a tunnel, near a door that opened as if by magic."

Thorn shook his head to clear it. "The last thing I remember is fighting the rats, and then I must have lost my footing. I'm grateful for your sending stone and sorry I lost it in the cave." He looked around. "Where is Raven?"

"Gone to fetch water for brewing a healing potion, but you seem well enough now."

"Aye, though my ears feel stuffed with wool."

Lira hurried about, picking up their belongings. "Raven says we must not wait for him, but go in search of the Lake of Fire."

Thorn glanced up. The sun nestled low in the trees, casting bars of cool shadow along the path. "It will be dark soon, but I do not have the rune stone the ancient one promised. Without it I cannot find the lake."

He got to his feet and tested his wobbly legs. "I must go back into the cave and find it."

Thorn had taken only a few steps when he spied on the ground the rough stone Lira had used for crushing her herbs. It was such an odd-looking thing that he picked it up and turned it over in his hand. At his touch it changed in hue from ordinary brown to deepest ruby, sparkling with light.

"Lira!"

"The rune stone! There is writing on it! Can you make out the words?"

"Morwid taught me many things, but not how to read," Thorn said.

Lira held the stone up to the light and turned it as she read, "'The sun is lost and no mortal can know where to find it. After ice and wind comes fire . . . and then the object of desire'!"

The sun is lost. Thorn went still, recognition dawning in his eyes. He *was* the sun seeker, just as Roger Tuckett had said on that long-ago morning on the road. The ruby stone pulsed and glowed in Lira's palm. More writing appeared.

"'Through the wood and through the brier, there to find the Lake of Fire,'" Lira read. She looked up. "We must go back the way we came, and right away, if we are to find the lake in time."

Thorn glanced around. "There must be some way around this cave."

"I don't see how," Lira said. "But without Raven I won't face those rats again." She shuddered.

"Look over that way," Thorn said, pointing to a green hill just beyond the clearing. "See if there is a path or a road. I'll look behind the cave."

They searched in silence for some minutes before Thorn's boot hit something hollow, and he bent to examine a long piece of dark wood hidden beneath a tangle of vines. "Lira!" he yelled. "Over here! A door!"

At his touch it opened with a loud *creak,* and they soon found themselves on a narrow road leading through a deep wood. Darkness was falling fast as they hurried through the forest. Beneath a cold and glittering moon they picked their way through the needle-sharp brier thicket and then onto a rutted path, a whirlwind of dry leaves tumbling in the air before them.

Presently Lira stopped and leaned against a tree, fighting for breath. "I cannot go another step. And my bones have turned to ice. I wish we had a cozy fire and something to eat."

"You shall have a fire at once, milady," said a voice in the dark.

"Raven!"

As if by magic, Raven appeared on the path carrying a brimming pot. "Your water, Princess, as promised. Though your twin hardly seems in need of it now."

"I don't need a healing potion," Thorn agreed, "but those herbs made my mouth dry as dust."

Raven handed Thorn the water pot. "I thought as much. I'm glad to see you are well, my friend. Lira and I feared for your life."

"So did I!" Thorn drank deeply of the cool water and wiped his chin. "Never have I faced anything as frightful as the Cave of the Wind."

"After the terrors of that cave the burning lake will not seem nearly so daunting," Raven said, kneeling to start a fire. "'Tis too bad we have nothing to eat, but at least we can slake our thirst and warm our weary bones."

When the water pot was empty, Lira and Raven fell into a tired heap beside the fire. Despite his exhaustion Thorn was too anxious for sleep. He lay quietly, trying to remember everything Morwid had taught him about swimming. Though he now understood why he feared the water, that knowledge did not make the task facing him any less daunting.

The sun is lost. Thorn turned the words over in his mind. Morwid had said the king wore the amulet about his neck. Perhaps, then, it was some kind of silken scarf woven of the finest golden threads. Or a thick chain with the image of the sun carved upon it. It was not at all clear to Thorn how possession of such an object would save his kingdom. But he had no choice except to trust Morwid's advice to be patient until the meaning was revealed.

He woke his companions and they continued down the trail. Here the air was heavy with the smell of damp earth and moss. Tendrils of fog crept along the ground. Slowly the sky lightened. Cresting a rise, Thorn glimpsed water and a glint of gold on the rim of the lake.

"The Lake of Fire," he murmured. "And somewhere beyond, the amulet."

"Your quest is nearly done," Lira said. "Soon R   ulf will be banished from our midst."

They reached the edge of the lake. White-hot flames

ringed the water, casting a pall of acrid smoke into the air. Whitecaps roiled on the dark surface. Through the smoke and flames Thorn glimpsed the opposite shore and a narrow patch of green leading away from the water's fiery edge. Fear tightened like a noose around his neck.

He opened his pouch and took out Morwid's remaining gift—the seashell.

Then the sudden drumming of horses' hooves sounded on the hill behind them.

"Someone is coming!" Raven shouted.

"Hide yourselves," Thorn yelled, "and wait for me!"

Then he dashed into the rim of fire. Flames licked at his doublet and singed his hair and eyelashes as he ran for the lake. He could feel the hairs on his arms withering. The air above the lake shimmered with heat. But his thoughts were clear. *The secret is to become one with the water.* He scooped water into Morwid's shell and drank it down.

A sudden calm filled his chest. He plunged into the water. His limbs felt loose and strong, and he struck out for the opposite shore. The water tumbled and roiled and gave off the cloying smell of rotting flowers. An arm's length down it was cooler, and he soon found it was easier to swim beneath the hot, restless surface. Again and again he dove and pushed through the water, his arms and legs slicing the waves.

Below the surface lay an enchanted world straight

out of one of Morwid's tales. Schools of bright yellow fish swam through an arch made of tiny shells that glowed pink and blue. A long skein of seaweed floated near the arch, seeming to beckon him closer. Thorn swam toward it and found a smooth white shell upon which a drawing had been carved. He scooped it up and kicked to the surface.

Treading water, he tucked the shell inside his doublet, then swam on and on across the vast lake, until at last his feet touched bottom. Standing waist deep in the water, he gulped air and studied the drawing on the shell. It was a map. He recognized the green patch of earth he'd spied from the far shore and the little dip in the shoreline that reminded him of a jagged bite taken from an apple. To his right a narrow path led to a spiral stone stair nearly hidden beneath tall green ferns and silvery moss. Once again Thorn raced through the ring of flames, then onward toward the stair.

In a dense grove of trees near the path to the lake, Raven and Lira crouched, watching as four horsemen halted their mounts on the hill high above them.

"I wish I had a spyglass," Lira whispered. "Can you tell who they are?"

"The ones who seek the amulet, no doubt." Raven shaded his eyes and squinted. "Stay here and wait for Thorn. I will find out."

"Watch how you go," Lira said. "And do not tarry. When Thorn returns with the amulet, we must go at once to Kelhadden."

"Aye." He grinned. "What a grand thing that will be."

Raven donned his cap and disappeared into the trees. Lira crept closer to the water's edge to watch for Thorn.

The path skirted a wide, dank-smelling marsh. Thorn raced over the grass, his feet scarcely touching the ground. Taking the stairs two at a time, he soon reached the top and halted there before a stone pillar upon which rested a glossy black cask.

The lid was secured by a carved gold clasp that yielded easily to his touch. He raked his wet hair from his eyes and ran his fingers over the satiny wood. He took a deep breath and opened the cask.

Beneath a thick layer of dust and cobwebs lay a golden chain encrusted with diamonds, rubies, and pearls. Suspended from the chain was a misshapen crystal sun nearly as large as Thorn's fist. Along one edge the glass was cracked, as if half the bauble had been broken off. Thorn lifted the treasure and placed it around his neck. The amulet settled onto his chest.

Jubilant, he spun around and shouted, "I have found it! I have found the sun!"

If only Morwid were here to witness the result of all

his labor! Thorn raised his arms and shouted, "I claim this amulet for the kingdom of Kelhadden!"

At his words the ring of fire vanished from the lake. The waves stilled; the surface shone smooth as glass. Across the valley he glimpsed sudden movement and a brief flash of light in the trees. Then he saw four horsemen riding pell-mell down the hillside, bearing straight for the glade where he'd last seen Raven and Lira.

He ran down the winding stairs and, without a moment's hesitation, plunged back into the lake. When he reached the far shore, Lira pulled him into the trees. "You found the amulet! Oh, it is the most beautiful thing. May I see it?"

"Not now. We are not alone in this wood. We must make at once for Kelhadden. Where is Raven?"

She handed Thorn his pouch, his bow and quiver. "Gone to see who was watching you from the top of the hill."

They hurried along the trail without finding any sign of the horsemen or Raven. Then as the light began to fade, Thorn spotted his friend running through the trees, his cloak in tatters, his feathered hat askew.

"I lost them!" Raven panted. "Four riders, armed to the teeth. I could not see which way they went." Then his thin face lit up as he spied the glittering pendant resting on Thorn's chest. "You have found the sun! Well done, my prince!"

Weak with hunger, his eyes gritty from lack of sleep, Thorn merely nodded and sagged against a large boulder that lay partially buried in the hillside. Now that his quest was done, he felt light-headed and hollowed out, as if he'd been stripped of muscle, blood, and bone.

"Sit down," Raven said, indicating a mossy spot in the clearing. "They will not find us here, and you must rest. On the morrow we will go home."

Thorn nodded. Despite his desire to return to Kelhadden as soon as possible, Raven was right. Thorn was too tired to go on. Taking the amulet from around his neck, he hid it in a deep crevice in the rock. "It will be safe here till we decide which way to go."

"If you wish, I will make a dream potion to show us the way home," Lira said. "I have everything I need. I am certain of it."

But Thorn shook his head. "I am through with potions. While you were gone, Raven mixed your herbs with the petals of Baldric's yellow flowers and that night I glimpsed something no mortal should see."

"Heaven?" Lira breathed.

"The future of mankind. It was a dream filled with great beauty, but also with unspeakable sorrow I could do little to change. I'd rather not speak any more of it."

"Aye," Raven said. "Despite its twists and turns, the future is better left to chance. Otherwise we would be too afraid to try anything." He handed Lira a pouch containing the last of that terrible potion. "I nearly lost this twice today while I was looking for the horsemen. You'd better take it for safekeeping. But don't pour it out just yet. It may prove useful before this quest is done."

Lira tucked the pouch inside her tunic, unsheathed her dirk, and began cutting kindling for a fire. Raven took Thorn's bow and arrows into the wood and presently returned with a hatful of berries and two fat quail. He set the birds on a spit and took out his flute. He was just about to begin a tune, when he remembered the horsemen they'd seen earlier in the day. "No music tonight," he decided. "We shall be quiet as mice until morning comes."

"If you please," Lira said with a shudder, "don't mention mice. Or rats. Horrid creatures!"

When the meat was brown and sizzling, Thorn devoured his portion in a few bites and licked his fingers clean. Now that he was rested and his hunger was satisfied, he felt better. "That is the tastiest meal I have ever eaten," he said to Raven. "Once we reach the castle, you will be not only my counselor, but chief cook as well."

"An excellent plan!" Lira said with a laugh.

"'Tis the company that makes the feast," Raven returned.

"The first thing I want when we get home is a warm

bath scented with oils, and a clean nightdress smelling of lilacs," Lira said dreamily. "Then I want a six-course dinner, starting with veal pasties, black pudding, and sausages. After that some salted eel and pea soup and a roasted capon with rice—"

"And a dessert of pears and nuts!" Thorn finished.

Raven chuckled. "I am honored you think me capable of producing such a feast, but methinks you will have more important plans to make once you are home."

"Aye." Thorn stood and began to pace in the clearing, his expression thoughtful. "First I must oust the Northmen and return the land to the forest people. They will need seeds for planting and sheep to replenish their flocks. The merchants and shopkeepers will need goods to sell."

"Some trader will pay a tidy sum for that jeweled chain," Lira said. "Even our mother's crown was not so richly adorned. Of course, Ranulf took that, and all else she owned, to build more of his loathsome warships. They still lie at anchor in our harbor, or so said the traveler whose clothes I borrowed the night I left the abbey."

"I won't trade away the jeweled chain," Thorn said. "It's an important part of the history of our kingdom. But I will have a new crown made for Mother."

"A garland of wildflowers will be enough," Lira declared.

Darkness had fallen. The fire burned low. "Stay here and rest," Lira said to her twin. "Raven and I will get more wood."

When they had gone, Thorn bent to warm his hands over the glowing coals. He felt numb, a stranger in his own skin. As impossible as it had seemed the day he left Morwid's cave, he had found the amulet. Soon he would be king. But the long road home still lay in front of him, and he was worried about the horsemen. He felt sure their presence in so remote a place was no coincidence. He left the fire and checked on the amulet once more, to be certain it was still safely hidden.

Behind him the dry grasses rustled. He spun around.

Ranulf strode into the clearing.

CHAPTER TWELVE

"AH," RANULF SAID WITH A TWISTED SMILE. "MORWID'S young protector. Where are your companions, boy?"

Raven crept soundlessly into the trees. Dirk in hand, Lira moved into the circle of firelight and stood beside Thorn. "Here I am, Father."

Ranulf's hard gaze rested first on Lira, then on Thorn. The Northman made a small sound that might have been a laugh, but it died in his throat. Thorn saw the flicker of apprehension in his father's eyes and remembered the old woman at March's inn who had been certain that twins portended evil.

He is afraid of us! Without thinking, Thorn sent this silent message to his twin and saw her nod in response.

"Well," Ranulf said, recovering himself. "It's the runaway sorcerer and the secret prince. It has been many a year since I saw you, Lira. I thought you dead by now. Tell me, have you cast any spells lately? Any circles of flame? Or has life with that prune-faced abbess dried up all your skills?"

"What do you want?" Thorn asked angrily. Seeing Ranulf again reminded him of the vicious attack on his teacher. Thorn could almost smell Morwid's skin burning beneath the cautery iron.

"Why, the amulet, of course. And do not bother to deny you have it. I followed you from the cave yestereve and watched you swim the lake to get it."

"When we met upon the trail the night you attacked Morwid, you did not know me," Thorn said. "Do you recognize me now, Father?"

"Don't you dare use that name with me!" Ranulf bellowed. "I renounce kinship to both of you, so doubly cursed. Born of a treacherous queen and on a night when the sky was red as blood."

"You are the treacherous one," Thorn and Lira said together.

Ranulf paled but went on. "When I first learned there were two of you, I nearly beheaded the dwarf for telling such a preposterous tale, but he soon convinced me it was true."

At that a familiar voice floated in from the trees.

"Oh, my sovereign, my honored king. You give me too much credit. Too much credit indeed."

"Baldric!" Lira cried.

"One and the same." The dwarf shuffled out of darkness leading a magnificent white horse. He bowed to the twins. "Ranulf was more than happy to meet my price for the dream potion and to give me this fine mount in the bargain. But when I told him where I saw you last, it was easy enough to discover your trail." He giggled and rubbed his hands together. "Soon he will have the amulet, and I shall be on my way to the kingdom my heart has long desired." He stroked the horse's head. "And in fine style, too. No more swinging through the trees for me. At last everyone will be happy. Well, not you two, of course, but—"

"Be quiet, you fool!" Ranulf's eyes glittered in the light. "Hand over the amulet, Thorn."

"I do not have it," Thorn said.

"Then we shall unearth every tree and stone to find it." Ranulf put his fingers to his lips and gave a piercing whistle. Instantly two other Northmen entered the clearing. Thorn recognized Trevyn and Olfar, the king's guards.

Olfar, the younger and shorter of the two, strode over to Thorn. "You are the arrogant little upstart who sent me over the cliff nearly to my death. I must admit, though, that Morwid taught you well the value of surprise."

"Morwid!" Ranulf spat the word as if it were a curse. "The world is better rid of that babbling lunatic."

Morwid lives! Thorn wanted to shout. But his mentor had also impressed upon him the value of silence. Better to let Ranulf think his attack on the old warrior had succeeded.

Olfar placed the cold, hard tip of his sword against Thorn's neck. "Where is the amulet?"

"Tell him nothing, Thorn!" Lira cried.

"Quiet, girl!" Trevyn grabbed her, tossed her dirk away, and held her fast.

Lira kicked his shins and jabbed his ribs with her elbows. "Let go of me!"

Baldric lurched about the clearing, ransacking their pouches, upending their packs, shaking out their cloaks. "The amulet *must* be here."

"Stop, you idiot!" Ranulf cried. "Even Thorn is smart enough not to leave so valuable a thing in plain sight. We'll have to search this wood from top to bottom."

"In the dark?"

"Make a torch, you dunderhead. Over there by that boulder lies a sturdy branch. Bring it here."

Thorn watched in growing fear as Baldric pushed past him and approached the boulder where the amulet lay hidden. He tried to slow his breathing lest Olfar sense his fright and discern the truth. His eyes sought

Lira's. Shouldn't they try to cast some spell to stop the dwarf? But Lira couldn't escape Trevyn's iron grasp. Thorn silently mouthed "Raven?" and Lira answered with an almost imperceptible shake of her head.

"Oh, my king, come quick!" Baldric shouted. "I have found something."

Thorn's shoulders slumped as Ranulf stalked to the boulder and peered into the deep crevice.

"By my bones!" the Northman said, drawing the jeweled amulet from its hiding place. "'Tis the missing sun at last, and it is even more magnificent than I dreamed." He held it up for the guards' inspection. "'Tis said its brilliance is dazzling enough to make even the darkest night turn bright as day. Now we'll see whether those claims be true."

He held the amulet to the firelight, turning it this way and that, but nothing happened. He strode over to Thorn. "What magic releases its power?" he demanded. "Speak quickly, boy, for I am weary and out of patience."

"I do not know," Thorn said truthfully.

Then Olfar shoved Thorn toward Ranulf just as Baldric planted himself firmly between the Northman and the young prince.

"Wait!" Baldric cried to Ranulf. "I have kept my part of the bargain. You have the amulet. Now I would have my gold coins and the map to the peaceful kingdom."

Ranulf rocked back on his heels and laughed. "The peaceful kingdom! You imbecile! Do you not know such a place is made only of wishes and dreams? Now, get out of my way."

"But, but . . ."

Enraged, Baldric stomped so hard on the king's foot that Ranulf bellowed, grabbed his foot, and dropped the glittering amulet. Olfar's sword clattered as he pushed Thorn aside and grabbed the sputtering dwarf.

"Put me down this instant!" Baldric yelled. The Northman laughed and held him at arm's length. The dwarf's feet churned in the air before Olfar let go and Baldric tumbled to the ground.

Thorn dived for the amulet and snatched it up just before Trevyn threw Lira aside, drew his sword, and rounded on Baldric. But Ranulf, with a terrible, casual swiftness, plunged his own sword deep into Baldric's chest. Lira screamed. The bloodied dwarf gasped and lay still. Then through the trees came the neighing of horses and the dull clank of heavy armor. A voice shouted, "Left flank, ready?"

"Ready!" came the answer from the opposite direction.

"What is this?" Ranulf spun around in the clearing, his shimmering red cloak fanning the campfire's dying embers.

"Right flank, ready?"

The two guards rushed to their king, poised for battle. "We are surrounded, Your Majesty!" Olfar cried. "Why, there must be an entire army out there."

"I told you we should have brought our own men," Trevyn said. "But you said 'tis only a boy we are after and—"

"Silence! Both of you!" Ranulf growled. "Go and see what army is out there, and come back here at once."

Trevyn and Olfar rushed into the forest. Ranulf, his own weapon still dripping with Baldric's blood, rounded on Thorn. "Give me the amulet."

In a trice Thorn looped the bejeweled chain over his head and held the crystal sun close to the firelight, hoping the amulet would indeed release its powerful light. But nothing happened.

Bewildered, he yelled to Lira, "It's useless. Run!"

Lira scooped up her dirk, tucking it into her tunic as they fled the clearing. Thorn grabbed her hand and they raced through the trees, leaping small boulders, twisting and turning in the darkness. Behind them came Ranulf, brandishing his bloody sword, his breath coming in hot gusts as he closed the gap between them.

Deeper into the forest the twins ran, until Lira tripped on a huge root and they both tumbled to the ground. Thorn lay breathless in the thick undergrowth, overcome with disappointment. Everything he had endured during his long and difficult quest seemed for naught. And now his own father was out for blood. For the first time Thorn wondered about Morwid. Did the old warrior truly believe in the Book of Ancients and its prophecies of princes and comets, or had he simply grown tired of Thorn and tricked him into embarking on a fool's errand?

"Thorn!" Ranulf shouted. "You may as well come out, for I will not leave until I have the amulet."

Lira removed the crystal necklace Thorn had noticed the morning he and Raven scaled the garden wall in search of bloodrose and balsam.

"Thief of light that goes by night—" she began.

"Shall with its twin restore the right," Thorn finished.

"Aye! The bard *must* have meant the moon!" Lira whispered. "It makes no light of its own, but takes its radiance from the sun."

Lira handed Thorn her necklace. "If we put the two halves together, sun and moon, perhaps then the amulet will work."

Half then whole, Thorn thought. His fingers trembled as he placed the bejeweled crystal sun next to Lira's moon. There was a small click as the two halves came together.

"Ah! There ye be!" Ranulf crashed through the thicket and fell upon the twins. Swords and dirks clattered as

Lira and Thorn fought him, turning this way and that, crouching behind boulders and trees, struggling to escape. Lira slashed their way through a tangle of vines, startling a flock of night birds, which rose and circled, calling in the dark. Then Olfar surprised them from behind and, with one savage thrust of his dirk, slashed Thorn's leather doublet and sent him sprawling into the dirt. Thorn felt blood soaking through his tunic. He rolled onto his back.

A moment later Ranulf was bending over Thorn, one meaty hand on his sword, the other grasping the amulet. Thorn could not have said just where he got the courage to spit in Ranulf's eye, an act so bold and unexpected that the Northman flinched and momentarily lowered his sword.

That single moment was all the time Thorn needed. He twisted away, leapt to his feet, and held the amulet aloft. "Thief of light that goes by night shall with its twin restore the right!" he yelled. "Sun and moon, upon this hour, descend with all your fearsome power!"

Then the entire forest blazed with a dazzling, unearthly brilliance that sent the Northmen to their knees. Olfar screamed and covered his eyes. Ranulf's hand trembled so furiously his sword slipped from his grasp and thumped into the dirt. He blinked and turned his face away, but the light held him fast, as surely as if he were in chains.

While Thorn grasped the shimmering amulet, Lira picked up their father's sword and stood beside her twin, pride and triumph shining in her eyes. Pointing the sword at the two Northmen, she said, "What shall we do with them, my prince?"

One blow from the sword, Thorn thought, and Ranulf would be dead and no longer a threat to Kelhadden. The deaths of countless countrymen, King Warn's shameful defeat, and Morwid's long, hard exile all would be avenged. But Thorn could not repeat the evils of his father, could not claim the throne with blood on his hands. "Tie them up," he said. "We will take them back to our camp."

And so, with the Northmen's own ropes, Lira bound both Ranulf and Olfar and linked them together at their waists. When Thorn bent to help her secure the knots, the king sneered. "Kill me if it pleases you. I would rather die a soldier's death than live a single moment as your captive."

"I will decide later what to do with you," Thorn said. "For now, I must find Raven."

They wound their way back through the forest, Thorn in the lead. Ranulf and Olfar, muttering vengeful oaths, shuffled along in their ropes behind him, and Lira brought up the rear.

No sooner had they regained the campsite than Trevyn burst into the clearing carrying an awkward bundle over his shoulder. "There was no army in that wood," he began hurriedly, "only a miserable urchin rattling our own horses' harnesses with his . . ."

Trevyn's voice trailed away at the sight of his king and countryman in ropes. He drew his broadsword and advanced toward Thorn, but Olfar yelled, "Stay back, unless you wish to join us. The amulet works only for the upstart princeling and his witch sister."

Trevyn stopped and called to Ranulf, "What happened, my lord?"

"What happened?" Ranulf bellowed. "We have been bested by these two evil ones and their dark magic. Had I known they were twins on the night of their birth, I would have drowned them both like stray cats and spared ourselves this trouble."

"Which is exactly why Mother sent Thorn to live with Morwid!" Lira said. "It seems you've been outsmarted yet again, Father!"

"Well, this one will not give you any more trouble," Trevyn declared. "He's dead." So saying, he dumped his bundle onto the ground.

A strangled cry escaped Thorn, a howl of rage that filled the wood.

"Raven!"

CHAPTER THIRTEEN

With her father's sword Lira held Trevyn at bay.
Thorn found Raven's rope and quickly bound Trevyn's
hands and feet. Then they both bent to their fallen
companion. In the firelight Raven's features were white
and smooth as stone. His dark hair lay curled against a
forehead already growing cold. Overcome with grief,
Lira cradled his head in her lap and sobbed.

"Is there nothing we can do?" Thorn asked, his
voice breaking. "Surely there is some chant, some spell
or potion that will bring him back."

Lira wiped her eyes. "With all my heart I wish it
were so, but my meager gifts are no match for death."
Then, seeing for the first time her twin's bloodstained

doublet, she said, "You are hurt! Let me tend your wound."

In the wake of their discovery of the amulet's power, and the loss of their friend, Thorn had forgotten his wound. Now his side throbbed painfully, but he said, "I am all right. This doublet deflected the blow."

The forest seemed eerily silent. The fire had burned to embers. A pale moon nestled in the bare branches. In the undergrowth the wild creatures burrowed or hunted or slept curled against their young, unmindful that death would one day overtake them. How lucky they were, Thorn thought bitterly, not to know the cruel fate that awaited them. Hot tears welled up inside him. Tears, aye, and a pain so sharp he was not certain he could bear it. A wave of fury began deep in his belly, rose to his chest, and stuck in his throat. He wanted to weep and scream his outrage to the world, but Ranulf's hard eyes were following his every move, and Thorn refused to let the Northman witness his grief. To hide his sorrow, he turned away and piled more wood onto the embers, then knelt and fanned them till the flame caught again.

Trevyn said to Ranulf, "The dead one surely was enchanted, Sir, for he could cast his voice in any direction. He was alone in the wood with our own mounts, tricking us into thinking an army awaited us there. But he has played his last trick."

"Stop your blathering!" Ranulf ordered. "Can you not see none of it matters now?"

Trevyn shifted his gaze to Thorn. "I suppose you mean to kill us."

"It would not bring Raven back," Thorn said, his voice cracking with feeling, "nor erase the evil you have done. But I mean to banish you from Kelhadden." To Lira he said, "Bring their mounts."

She left the clearing and soon returned with their horses. Thorn said to the guards, "Do you still swear fealty to Ranulf?"

"To the death!" they answered.

"Then go at once to Kelhadden. Say that the prince will return anon. Then round up your countrymen, every man, woman, and child, and bid them board the warships fouling my harbor. Sail to the summer country, to the place where the river meets the sea. I will meet you there in three days' time and hand over your king."

Lira pinned the guards with her gaze. "You have already seen the power of the amulet. You would be wise to do as my brother says."

Thorn nodded. "My twin is a seer. So even though you travel beyond my mortal gaze, she will know your every move."

Olfar's eyes bulged. He nodded. "Aye. Dark magic."

"Three days," Thorn reminded them. "Not one hour more."

"But . . . but," Trevyn sputtered. "That is impossible! It will take twice that long to gather our belongings and make ready to sail."

"Your belongings? None of it is yours."

"But—" Olfar began.

"Quiet!" Ranulf cried. "Do as he says, for I would not spend another day in the company of this arrogant child."

"You are the arrogant one, Father," Lira said, handing the reins to Thorn.

"I would not claim a witch as my daughter."

"I would sooner be the daughter of a snake," Lira retorted. "I will admit I had little use for Baldric, but he did not deserve to die merely for demanding his part of your bargain."

Ranulf shrugged. "He walks in the peaceful kingdom at last."

Unsheathing his dirk, Thorn severed the ropes binding the king's guards. "Go now. I will watch for your ships from the bluff above the river."

"And I," said Lira to the guards, "will be watching *you!*"

Trevyn bowed to Ranulf, though the king was seated rather unceremoniously on the ground. "Do not trouble your mind, my lord, for I will return as promised, and we shall find new kingdoms to conquer."

When the two guards were gone, Lira searched

Ranulf's belongings and found more food than either of the twins had seen in a very long time—bread and honey, venison and pickled eel, pears and plums, and a tin of sugared nuts. But neither she nor Thorn could eat a bite. Ranulf lay in a disheveled heap, his hands folded over his belly. Soon he fell into a twitchy sleep and began to snore.

Thorn sat beside Raven, wanting to be near his fallen friend.

Lira began to keen softly. "I will miss him so!"

She touched Raven's cheek, but Thorn couldn't bring himself to look upon his companion, for fear he would later remember Raven dead and not alive. Instead Thorn watched the rise and fall of his father's chest. In sleep the Northman did not seem quite so fierce. "What makes a man become as cruel as our father?" he wondered aloud. "Was he always so full of spite?"

Lira wiped her eyes and sniffed. "Like your Morwid, our father is a puzzlement. One moment he is gentle as an April breeze, the next he is seething with rage. One evening when I was no more than three or four, I fell so terribly sick with a fever Mother feared I would not last until morning. Father sat by my side all night making poultices for cooling my brow. When I was better, he brought red ribbons for my hair."

"I cannot imagine such kindness in him."

"His tender feeling was but a fleeting thing," Lira said. "Later that same afternoon he seized a bulrush and poked out the eye of the hapless stable boy who arrived late with Father's favorite mount. Mother was beside herself, but there was nothing we could do."

As Lira talked on, it seemed to Thorn that the darkness might go on forever, but at last the sun rose over the valley. The mist lifted; birdsong gradually filled the wood. Numb with grief, Thorn sat unmoving beside Raven's body.

"Thorn," Lira said gently. "It is time to lay him to rest."

A new wave of sorrow, deep as a death wound, washed over Thorn. The tears he had tried so hard to hold at bay rolled unchecked down his face. "I cannot."

"You must. In three days' time we will hand over this sorry excuse for a ruler, then make for home. You must think now not of your own broken heart, but of your duty to your people."

Reluctantly Thorn rose. The twins woke Ranulf and bound him fast to a tree. Then they wrapped Raven in his cloak and carried him to a wooded hillside overlooking the lake.

"The ground is too hard for digging a grave," Thorn said, "even if we had a proper tool." He choked back a sob. "The best we can do is to leave him here beneath these trees."

"Raven won't mind," Lira said gently.

Thorn placed Raven's flute atop his chest, but Lira could not bear to part with his hat. She settled it upon her own head. The black feather glistened in the morning light.

"Destiny required him to give his life in your service, and he gave it gladly," Lira said. Then she revealed Raven's secrets from their shared evening beside the fire.

"Raven was the grandson of the seer Drucilla?" Thorn asked, incredulous.

"Aye. And completely calm in the face of the sacrifice he was fated to make. He was only partly mortal," Lira related, "and he did not fear death. He would not want us to mourn, but to finish our task with bravery and honor."

"Even so, I can't bear to think I will never see him again." Thorn took a long, shuddering breath. "I shall never meet a finer friend in this world or the next."

Thorn meant to turn and go then, before the pain overtook him, but even the vast wood seemed too small to contain his grief. He stood beside Raven, wracked with sobs, waiting for something to change inside him, something that would make it possible to leave his friend lying there so still and alone, so far from the green hills of Kelhadden. But there was nothing but a numb emptiness that threatened to overwhelm him.

Lira took his hand. Despite all her years in the abbey, she could think of no words of solace for her brother. "Come away now. Lingering here will only prolong our sadness."

"Aye. A king cannot afford self-pity. But I shall miss him every day of my life." Thorn removed a carved bone button from his tattered doublet and placed it gently on Raven's chest. "Rest well, Galystawen."

"He is safe," Lira murmured. "Let's go."

They returned to the clearing to find Ranulf sleeping again, his head falling forward onto his chest. Nearby, Baldric's body lay across the path.

"We cannot leave him here like this," Lira said.

"Agreed. We'll lay him over there beneath that tree and cover him with his cloak."

When that was done, the twins prepared for their journey. While Thorn doused the fire and readied the horses, Lira gathered their father's cloak, his spyglass and sword, and his bulging leather packs. "At least we will eat well on this journey," she said to Thorn.

"Aye." Thorn finished his preparations, then shook his father's shoulder. "Wake up. Time to go."

"Not a moment too soon," Ranulf grumbled as Thorn worked to free him from the tree. "Untie my feet, boy, so that I may mount my horse."

"Lira and I will lift you, and you can ride sidesaddle."

"I will not ride like a woman!" Ranulf said.

"As you wish." Thorn's brows went up in a question and he shot Lira an amused look. Two pairs of amber-colored eyes met and held. She nodded her agreement.

"Stop that!" Ranulf shouted.

"Stop what?" Thorn winked at his twin.

"Talking without words. Reading each other's minds. It's unnatural."

Thorn ignored that. "On three," he said to Lira. "Ready?"

"One, two, three!" Lira said, and the twins tossed Ranulf across the back of his horse facedown, where he lay graceless as a sack of potatoes.

Thorn bent to his father. "Comfortable, Your Majesty?"

"The devil take you."

"Someday mayhap he will, but I hope not today," Thorn said mildly.

Then, because he had never before ridden a horse, Lira showed Thorn how to hold the reins and how to guide the horse with the pressure of his knees. They set off, riding together on Baldric's white mount, their father jouncing along beside them on his own black stallion.

As the day lengthened, Thorn described for Lira the ancient being on the mountain, her strange cave with its pots and herbs and spinning wheel, her red-eyed lizard, and the clues she had given him to help him in his quest. "Though I know it cannot be so, I felt almost as if I knew her."

"The world is full of magic," Lira said. "Stranger things have happened."

"What a lot of idiotic blather," Ranulf muttered when Thorn stopped for breath. "Do you never stop your senseless chatter?"

Lira said, "I think Thorn's story is quite wonderful. Almost like a fairy tale. If it bothers you, Father, shut your ears. Go ahead, Thorn. Tell me more."

At the bottom of the hill the road veered sharply, and they entered a tunnel of trees. Here the air was cool and still, the silence broken only by the sound of the horses' hooves on the hard ground and by Thorn's calm voice recounting his experiences on the icy mountain.

Presently the trail widened and they came first to a marsh and then to a clear stream surrounded by tall grasses. Exhausted by the events of the day, the twins quickly made camp. They helped Ranulf dismount, and after a meal of venison and fruit the twins prepared for sleep. Soon the Northman began snoring.

"Listen to him," Lira said. "He sounds like an old snuffling pig."

"A huntsman's horn," Thorn said.

Lira raked her hair from her eyes and stretched her legs toward the fire. "Once, he fell asleep while accompanying Mother and me on a picnic. Mother showed

208

me how to make him play a tune in his sleep. Watch."

She plucked a thick blade of grass, split it with her thumbnail, then held it a certain way just under Ranulf's mouth. With each breath the grass made a rhythmic, high-pitched squeak. *Scree-screep. Scree-screep.*

Ranulf sneezed, then snorted and rolled onto his side.

"Not nearly so tuneful as Raven's flute," Thorn said.

"No. Raven was one of a kind."

"His name will be honored in Kelhadden forever," Thorn said. "I shall see to it."

And with that, he slept.

The next day passed much as the first, with Thorn and Lira chattering like magpies, and Ranulf rousing himself every so often to utter a derisive snort or inject a harsh word or two. At midmorning on the third day they crested a hill and saw in the distance the shining river.

"Well?" Ranulf queried, twisting his neck into an awkward knot for a better view. "Do you see my ships, boy?"

"Nothing yet."

For most of the morning they waited with no sign of the ships. Thorn began to wonder whether it had been wise to trust Olfar and Trevyn to return for their king, and just what he would do with Ranulf if the Northman's kinsmen didn't come to claim him. He was quite relieved when at last he spotted movement on the horizon. Thorn raised Ranulf's spyglass to his eye. Under full sail seven ships were headed down the river, each of them brimming with men, women, and children, with sheep and dogs, with wooden barrels lashed haphazardly to the deck. "Here they come!" he cried.

"Deliverance at last!" Ranulf muttered.

As the lead ship reached a bend in the river, two men launched a skiff and made for the shore, where Thorn and Lira waited with their father. When the boat touched bottom, Thorn cut the ropes binding Ranulf's ankles.

"Your Majesty!" the oarsmen cried.

Ranulf acknowledged them with a grunt and an impatient wave of his hand, then climbed into the stern of the boat. One of the men jumped into the water, pushed the boat off the sand, then jumped into the skiff again. It rocked and settled, and the men bent to their oars.

As the boat moved away, Thorn could contain himself no longer. Cupping his hands around his mouth, he shouted, "Ranulf!"

The disgraced king showed no sign of having heard.

"Morwid lives!"

"Good riddance!" Lira said, rummaging through

Ranulf's packs. "Are you hungry? I am famished! And there are still plenty of good things to eat. Let's make an outing of it. After all the trouble we have endured, we deserve a feast."

She pointed to a sunny bluff situated higher above the river. "Up there. We can look all the way out to the sea."

They walked to the bluff, tethered their horses, and spread Baldric's blanket upon the ground. While they munched sugared nuts and golden pears, Thorn studied the map he'd found in the Northman's pack.

"Look at this." With his finger he traced a faint brown line. "I planned to return home through the summer country, but if this map be true, through that forest just over there is a bridge spanning the river, and a road that will bring us much sooner to the castle." He paused. "I wonder why Morwid never spoke of it."

"It does not matter now," Lira said happily. "All roads lead home. I cannot wait to see Mother again." She picked up the spyglass and idly scanned the river, the forest, and the valley far below.

"I am eager to see Morwid," Thorn said. "Despite his bluster and his secrets, and the hard tasks he set for me, I have missed him."

Lira put a hand on her brother's arm. "Someone is coming."

"A Northman?" Thorn reached for his dirk and tucked the amulet inside his doublet.

Frowning, Lira said, "Not a Northman. A fisherman, I think. His breeches and cloak are sopping wet."

"Let me look." Thorn raised the spyglass. He gasped, then scrambled to his feet and raced down the path, his long legs churning, his yellow hair streaming out behind him.

"Thorn! Wait! What . . ."

"Morwid!"

Lira ran down the hill behind her brother. Thorn soon reached the old warrior and with a joyous shout threw himself into Morwid's arms with such force they both nearly toppled off the ledge.

"Lira!" Thorn cried. "Come and greet the one who all my life has been both teacher and father to me."

Morwid disentangled himself and trained his rheumy gaze on Lira. "No wonder Drucilla complained she was seeing double, for you are as alike as grains of sand. Two as one. Indeed."

Thorn clung to his mentor, his mind whirling. "Has your wound healed, Teacher? How did you know where to find me? How could you come so far?"

"When Ranulf's men arrived with your orders to abandon the castle, I stowed away on one of their ships," Morwid said, "then jumped overboard at the bend in the river and swam ashore."

Morwid looked quite pleased with himself, but

Thorn said, "You are far too old for such things. And now you are shivering with cold."

"I have lived through worse," Morwid said as they started up the hill. "Much worse."

"Nevertheless," Thorn retorted, "it was not necessary to come for me."

"Do not lecture me, boy." Morwid's expression went hard. "You were gone so long I grew tired of waiting."

"You forget yourself, Sir," Lira said, her eyes flashing. "My brother is no longer your pupil, but your king."

Morwid gave her a baleful stare and grunted. When they reached the bluff, he looked around anxiously. "Where is the amulet?"

"Though the dream potion Drucilla gave me was stolen," Thorn said, "and we could not discern how to make more of it, with the help of your gifts and my brave allies I found it."

"Well done! I have waited a lifetime for this moment. May I see it?"

As if bestowing a gift, Thorn took the glittering treasure from inside his doublet and placed it in Morwid's hands.

"Ah," Morwid said. "It is a beautiful thing, the way it catches the light. 'Tis much heavier than I imagined, but its weight will be no burden to me."

A wave of foreboding passed through Thorn. "What do you mean?"

Morwid flashed a brittle smile. "For years it was I who managed the affairs of the kingdom. I have lost count of the worrisome nights spent alone in my chambers, pondering some weighty problem while your spineless grandfather slept like a babe in his warm bed. Since his death I have waited for the one thing that would allow me to claim my just reward. But until you were delivered into my safekeeping, I had no hope of finding it."

"Your reward?" Thorn asked. "You told me King Warn was a kind and generous king. I thought you loved him."

"I loved him well enough, and I mourned him when he died. 'Tis true he was a kindly soul, but he was weak and impulsive, unfit to rule a piggery." Morwid's blue eyes, which had so often regarded Thorn with kindness, now were cold and without expression. "You are just the same, Thorn. Too full of fears and questions to reign over an entire kingdom. As the twig is bent, so grows the tree."

"He is not the same!" Lira said fiercely. "A weak king could not slay a two-headed beast, climb a mountain of ice, brave a fearsome cave, or swim a lake of fire, but Thorn did!"

It was true. Thorn knew he was a different boy from the one who had set out from the sea cave weeks before. At the start of his quest he had been naive, untested, and afraid to trust his own judgment. Since then he had learned about facing fear, about wrong decisions, dead ends, and false assumptions. He knew his place now. Knew he had earned the right to the throne.

Thorn said, "The Book of Ancients says I am to be king."

Morwid snorted. "It says whoever shall possess the amulet will be king. And now I have it."

"I trusted you!" Thorn cried. "And this is how you repay me after I saved you from Ranulf and his guards?"

"You flatter yourself, boy. Do you believe you could have defeated three burly Northmen if they'd truly meant to kill you? Our encounter with them did not happen by chance."

With sudden clarity Thorn remembered the night Morwid took him to Drucilla's hut and then to the camp of the forest people. He remembered the pile of twigs Morwid so casually left on the stump in the orchard.

"You left Ranulf a sign so he'd know where to find us!"

Lira folded her arms across her chest. "You must have wanted the amulet very badly to allow Ranulf to inflict such a serious wound."

"I would do anything to possess the amulet,"

Morwid said, "but I will admit Ranulf's blow was more painful than I expected."

Thorn fought the tears welling in his eyes. In a voice laced with contempt and disbelief he said, "You conspired with our sworn enemy to steal my birthright?"

"He agreed to let me return to the castle as a servant in exchange for the amulet."

"After everything you taught me about honor and a warrior's pride," Thorn said, "I cannot imagine you as servant to anyone."

"I had a new potion," Morwid admitted, "more powerful than any other, to make Ranulf sleep as deeply as if he were dead. Taking the amulet from him then would have been easier than taking milk from a babe."

"Then Ranulf struck a bargain with Baldric for my dream potion in hopes of finding the amulet first." Thorn shook his head as if to clear his jumbled thoughts. "I can hardly believe it!"

"I'm not one bit surprised," Lira declared. "There is no honor among thieves."

Thorn said to Morwid, "You knew I wouldn't refuse the quest once I saw the misery of the forest people and witnessed your own suffering."

"Drastic measures were required," Morwid said. "Otherwise you would still be lolling about my cave disturbing my solitude, wasting time with your endless questioning and dithering."

"Drucilla warned me of another who sought the amulet," Thorn said. "You were so clever even she couldn't see that you were the one." He swallowed the hard knot pulsing in his throat, thinking how quickly his love and admiration for his teacher had turned to utter disdain. "At first I suspected Raven, and then Lira—everyone but you! Every word you spoke was a lie."

"Any fool can tell the truth," Morwid said, turning the amulet over in his hands. "But it takes a man of some cleverness to lie convincingly. And a clever king is precisely what Kelhadden needs at this hour."

"Aye. A clever king," Thorn murmured, his expression thoughtful.

Morwid held the amulet to the light, studying it from every angle. "Though it is quite lovely, I cannot divine how it works. What chant or spell releases its power?"

"I do not know, Teacher."

"Oh, stop calling me that. It grows tiresome." Morwid swung around to Lira. "Your father says you are a sorcerer of sorts. Tell me what I want to know, witch."

"Your Book of Ancients does not reveal the answer?" Lira's amber gaze held Morwid's. "It doesn't take magic to see that this amulet works only for the one who is meant to have it. It would not yield to Ranulf, and it will not yield to you. You may as well give it back."

"I must have it!" Morwid cried, his whole body trembling. "All those years of waiting and planning cannot have been for naught."

"Please, Sir," Thorn said. "So long as I have the amulet, our kingdom will be safe from the likes of the Northmen. Think of all the friends you have lost because of Ranulf's cruelty. Surely you want to end such suffering."

"Think of your friend Drucilla," Lira urged, "and our mother, who sacrificed her own happiness to spare you a life in the dungeon."

"I would never have been in the dungeon in the first place if your grandfather had listened to me. Don't come any closer, Thorn."

Kelhadden needs a clever king. Thorn sent Lira his thought. She met his gaze and nodded.

"Very well," Thorn said to Morwid with a resigned sigh. "The amulet works not by chant or spell, but by a potion so powerful the merest bit of it is all that is required."

Morwid regarded the twins through narrowed eyes. "The Book of Ancients says nothing about a potion."

Lira opened her pouch and took out the mixture Raven had concocted from herbs and the yellow flowers from the Valley of Sighs. "Here it is. But be careful. Don't swallow too much."

Morwid grabbed the pouch, opened it, and sniffed.

"A potent one, is it? Well, then, let us see what powers this amulet holds."

The old man scooped up a handful of the mixture and swallowed it.

Thorn and Lira waited anxiously. In a few moments beads of sweat formed on Morwid's forehead. His face reddened and his eyes bulged. He began running in circles, babbling oaths and uttering strange words.

"Evil and doom!" he cried. "Spirits of the sea and air! Help me!"

Still holding tightly to the amulet, Morwid clapped his hands over his ears and stumbled toward the rocky ledge that jutted above the roiling river. Before Thorn could catch him, the old warrior lost his footing and the amulet slipped from his grasp. With a startled cry Morwid tumbled down the rocky cliff and toppled into the river.

The amulet spun in the air and landed at Thorn's feet, the diamonds and rubies on the golden chain winking in the light. Thorn grabbed it and peered over the edge of the cliff just in time to see Morwid's body disappear into the racing current.

After a long silence, broken only by the rushing of the river, Lira placed her hand on her twin's arm. "Now your quest is truly ended."

"I wish it had never come to me," Thorn said fiercely. "I wish I had never heard of Morwid or the

Book of Ancients or this blasted amulet. Now Morwid is dead and it's my fault."

"No, his greed was his undoing. If he'd taken only a bit of the potion, he might have slept, and then we could have taken back the amulet. But he swallowed too much and it drove him mad. You are not to blame."

"I hate him!" Thorn cried. "I thought he meant to help the forest people. But he wanted the amulet for himself."

"Nothing hurts more than betrayal. But think of all that would be lost in years to come if you hadn't found the amulet."

"I have lost two fathers in one day."

"One of them was never worth your tears. And Morwid proved faithless in the end." Lira kissed her brother's cheek. "No good can come from mourning the past."

"Aye." Thorn squared his shoulders. "We must think of the future. There is much to be done."

"Come," Lira said. "Let's go home."

CHAPTER FOURTEEN

FOLLOWING THE MAP THORN HAD FOUND AMONG THEIR father's things, the twins rode through the forest, clattered across the wooden bridge, and took the road that wound upward from the valley. And so it was that after several days' journey, on a morning filled with sunshine and gentle breezes, they crested the hill. Through the distant trees rose the castle at Kelhadden, shimmering above the sea mist like something in a dream.

"There it is!" Lira breathed. "I despaired of ever seeing Kelhadden again."

Thorn nodded. His homecoming was not at all the way he had imagined it—with Raven riding triumphantly at his side and Morwid waiting on the road to greet him, the Book of Ancients hidden beneath his billowing cloak.

"You are remembering Raven," Lira said, reaching out to touch her twin's sleeve. "There is no shame in being sad, but I beg you not to forget your teacher's words. There is so much to be done." She glanced at the sky. "If we hurry, we can be home by sundown."

"Home," Thorn said. "Your stories of life in the castle with our mother make it seem almost familiar. I will be happy to see it for myself."

"You have earned the right to call Kelhadden home," Lira said.

"Then let's not waste any more time."

"If these horses had wings, the journey would still be too slow to suit me," Lira said, smiling. "But truth to tell, my brother, we look a fright."

Beside a rushing stream they rested the horses and washed away the grime of their journey. With a silver-backed brush she'd found in Ranulf's pack Lira smoothed and braided her hair and fastened the end with a length of flowering vine. She settled Raven's feathered hat on her head. "There. I am ready."

Thorn brushed the tangles from his own hair, shook the pebbles from his boots, and beat the dust from his well-worn doublet. On his chest the crystal amulet, sun and moon, winked and glittered. "How do I look?"

"A little worse for wear," Lira said truthfully. "But

very brave. Brave and wise and altogether magnificent. You will serve our kingdom well."

They mounted their horses and cantered along the road. As they neared the castle, they could hear the sounds of people cheering and the music of the wildly tumbling church bells. One by one the forest people emerged from their hiding places and stood along the road to the castle, eager for a glimpse of their new king. A ragged girl ran into the road and offered Thorn a curtsy and a bouquet of wildflowers. Then a barefoot woman in a worn cloak stepped into the road. She bowed her head and a bit of dried seaweed tumbled from her hair. As she brushed it from her face, Thorn saw that she wore a thistle bracelet.

"Mother!" Lira leapt from her horse and threw herself into the woman's arms. "Despite everything, you are as beautiful as ever!"

"Five years in hiding have left me changed."

"You are not changed. You are just the same, and I am so happy to be home."

Their mother laughed. Thorn sat astride Ranulf's black stallion trying not to feel envious of all the years his twin had spent with their mother, years that were lost to him forever.

"Thorn!" Lira cried as the crowd of well-wishers pressed closer. "Come and meet our mother."

He slid from his mount, bowed, and said simply, "Mother."

The word tasted strange and honey sweet on his tongue. "Mother, I wish I could have been with you all my life."

"You have been, my son."

Thorn knew then that it was true. Though he couldn't explain how she had done it, he understood that in the moments when he had felt most abandoned, afraid, and alone, somehow his mother had been there all the time, guiding him. Enfolded now in her tight embrace, he felt not like a hero or a king, but like an ordinary boy, adored and happy, and home at last.

His mother touched the shining amulet on his chest. "You have found the sun. Well done."

Thorn gazed at his mother, a thousand questions forming on his tongue.

"Later we will speak of many things," she said as the crowd swelled, "but now a celebration awaits at the castle."

"But . . ." Thorn stammered. "You . . . how?"

Lira caught her brother's arm and twirled him around in a merry little dance. "You want to know how she did it. But some mysteries are best left unsolved. Let's eat. I am famished."

Their mother laughed. "You must not expect too much, Lira. Though the Northmen left behind more food than we have seen in many years, this day's feast is hardly worthy of a king."

"Whatever is there will be shared by all," Thorn declared.

At that, the ragtag crowd cheered again. Thorn helped his mother onto his mount, and with Lira they rode to the castle gate. Behind them came the ravaged people of Kelhadden, sick, hungry, and hollow eyed after their long exile. Looking into their expectant upturned faces, Thorn understood that in the days to come his most important duty as king was not to restore their fields and orchards, though that was important, but instead to restore their faith in themselves and their king.

"It will take a very long time to undo the damage the Northmen have caused," he said to his twin. "Where should we begin, Counselor?"

They halted their horses beneath the trees. Lira touched the moonstone, the symbol of trust between counselor and king since ancient times. "I must return the coins to Saint Anne's. The abbess will have need of them."

"Lira!" their mother said. "Surely you did not steal from the church."

"I only borrowed them. And for a most worthy cause. The abbess will not mind one whit when she learns we are rid of the Northmen."

Thorn said, "The people must have food and shelter. We'll make room for them in the castle until they can repair their houses."

"Then we must get the Book of Ancients from Morwid's cave," Lira advised. "For it holds all we need to know of what is past and what is yet to be."

So saying, she opened her leather pouch and poured the last bit of Raven's yellow potion into her palm. Thorn nodded, his gaze steady on hers.

Lira opened her fingers and with a single breath blew it all away.